Love
&
Consequences

A novel by Nyema

Copyright © 2006 by Nyema M. Taylor

ISBN 978-0-9791138-0-2

Cover design created by QBS Designs
Edited by Charlene Bapttista
Text formation by Anna K. Stone

Published by Dreams 2 Write Publishing
For more information email: taylor.nyema@comcast.net
   www.nyemataylor.com

Printed in the United States of America
Printed on Recycled Paper

This Book is dedicated to my son, Shamir Jr. and the following loved ones not here with us today:

<u>R.I.P</u>

Jay-Roc

Pop Pop

Emily

Kandi

Minnie

Betty

Eric

Kassim

Pudgie

Carrie

I love you all and may God bless your souls…

ACKNOWLEDGEMENTS

First and foremost, I would like to thank my heavenly father for making this all possible for me.

My husband, my soul mate, my best friend. You were there day and night looking over my shoulder to correct the wrong and applaud the right. I love you more than words could ever say or show.

Mom, you are my idol and best friend. Thanks for showing me the way and giving nothing but support. I love you with all my heart and soul. Dad, without you I wouldn't be who I am today and I love you for that. I can't leave out the one who helped raise me into the intelligent woman I am today, my stepfather David Crawford, thanks for all the love and strict guidance. Ms. Sharmaine, it took some time but its here boo so thanks for the love. To both Grandmas Dee and Nell, I love you to death and nothing will ever change that.

Thanks to all my brothers, sisters, aunts, uncles, cousins, nieces, nephews and friends that been standing behind me since day one. Nell and Kesha, thanks for being a part of this and making the cover look hot. Luv ya'll.

Thanks to the whole Star Track Staff & Family, my Jersey family, my down south GA family, GIODT Entertainment, Mystique Hair Salon, Dreamchasers and EMPIRE Books. There aren't enough pages to name everyone and express how thankful I am to have your support, but I thank you from the bottom of my heart.

Kim, we cousins by blood but sisters at heart. You know I will have ya back til the end. Moe, you inspired me to write. I will be here for you forever. Nema, thanks for showing me the ropes and unconditional love. A sister ain't a sister if it ain't you. Yetta, thanks for the advice and being the loyal friend you are. Mirah, Jessica, Nina and Tasha, I love you all like blood. Bernice and Lashawnda, I'm loving ya'll from a distance!

To my extended family. I couldn't have chosen a better one. Mom Jack, Beat, Bruce, Deb, Kia and Sho'Nuff. You all took me in from the start and made me feel loved. Thanks for being there and showing nothing but support.

I wanna give special thanks to a few of my favorite people: JM Benjamin for helping me put together the last pieces to my puzzle, Yvonne Bridges and Black & Nobel Bookstore for lending a hand, Paula Edwards and Antoine McAdoo for all the good advice, Nakea Murray for hipping me to the game and Charlene Bapttista for taking the time to edit my work.

Last but not least, to all my promoters and supporters, thanks for helping me accomplish my goals. Words can never show how much I truly appreciate all the love and assistance. Thank You!

Chapter 1

DA JUMP OFF

I t was June 19, 2000, a couple days after graduation. West Catholic High obtained my study rights for the last four years and I was glad to be out. Summer was just blooming and I was anxious to get it over with so I could head off to college and meet my dream lover, future husband, or at least somebody to get my mind off the no good men out in the streets of Philadelphia.

For the last five years, I played major niggas wit major paper. My 5'5 frame, thick thighs, apple round bottom and flawless brown skin tone made it easy. All I had to do was lick my soft butter lips and gaze at them with my hazel brown eyes and they were drooling over my body like teething infants. The age didn't matter. I had young guys and old heads spending mad money on this beautiful creature. If they were under eighteen, I played my normal age. If they were a little older, then I too was a little older. My maturity hid it all. But, they say what goes around comes around, and that couldn't be truer.

I was going on nineteen at the present time. Three years back, the unexpected happened. I was the one to fall victim. His name was Slim. He taught me and did things to me that no one had ever done. That's why I loved him. The bad part is, the love was only one sided. He was tall, bald and sexy. He knew how to work every position to perfection. Not only physically, but also mentally. He had my head messed up and took full advantage. After a while, I started to get

1

approached by different females, harassed on my cell phone, and caught him in action on several different occasions. That still didn't make me leave. I cried and prayed asking for a way out. Soon after, he was gone. Locked up doing a two-year bid. That's when I cleared my head focusing on nothing but school.

Knowing the last couple of months in Philly was gonna be long ones, I prepared myself best I could for the adventure.

I was in the middle of a good dream lying in the arms of Morris Chestnut when the phone rang. "Yes," I answered, with a groggy voice.

It was my cousin Kizzy, who knew just how to mess up a wet dream. "Skyy, get up!"

"What the hell do you want? It's only eight in the morning, girl."

"Get up," she whined. "We gotta get on our jobs early!"

"I'm gonna move on your ass soon as I see you. Bye!"

"No wait!" she shouted, stopping me from ending the call. "I'm about to pick up Armani and Mashae so be ready."

"For *what*?"

"So we can get ready to hit the mall. You know tonight is big for all of us."

"The mall doesn't open 'til ten. What you so in a rush for?"

"You of all people need a head start," Kizzy spat.

"Look, call me back in thirty minutes. I'm tired."

"Why? Who you trick last night?" she joked.

"Your man. So bye," I sarcastically responded.

2

"Alright whore, but we'll be over there soon."

That's how we talked to each other. Really didn't mean anything by it, but true friends already know not to get offended. I tried to close my eyes and catch some more zzzs, but of course the phone rang again.

"What is it now?" I answered, snobbishly.

"Well, that's no way to talk to somebody you suppose to be interested in."

My mouth fell open so wide you could have stuck an apple in it. It was Key, the star forward for Duke University. Not only was he scouted to the big leagues, but he was also a sexual chocolate drop that could sure enough to cure my sweet tooth. I met him last night down at *Chrome Night Club* on Delaware Ave. Mashae, Kizzy, Armani and I decided to go to the club at the last minute because there wasn't anything else to do.

"Hello, are you still with me?" he asked, wondering if I had hung up.

"Yeah, I'm here," I stated, trying to get my thoughts together.

"You sound surprised to hear my voice. What? You thought I was lying when I said I'd call you?"

"Well, when you said you would, I didn't think it would be at eight-thirty in the morning."

"I was wondering if I could take you out for breakfast."

I wanted to jump up and down, but you know I had to keep my cool. One thing I had learned if I didn't learn anything else is not to jump at a nigga with money. They're the ones looking for a challenge, so I concealed my excitement. "That would have been nice if I didn't have something else to do."

"Oh, I see. You're trying to play that role, huh?"

I guess guys just knew when females were pulling their chains, or shall I just say frontin'. "And what role is that?"

"The *don't think I'm on you* role," he humbly replied.

"Whatever! I said I have business to tend to," I hissed.

"Yeah, you right. It's your call not mines," he smirked. "I guess I holla at you another time."

Come pick me up right now and I'll give you whatever you want, is what I wanted to say, but instead replied, "I guess so."

"Nice talking to you anyway."

"Dido," I said, before hanging up to make sure I got the last word.

I could hear in his voice that he wasn't use to rejection, and wasn't too sure if I would ever hear from him again.

This party better be the hell worth it, I thought while imagining that sexy, chocolate forward I had just brushed off. *What's the matter with you Skyy? That could be the one.*

I had that problem a lot. Always settling down thinking I found the right one and they turned out to be knuckleheads. He probably had some slick shit up his sleeve anyway. As I went to get up the phone rang again.

"Are you up yet? Kizzy just got here. We're on our way," asked Armani, my other pain in the neck cousin.

"I'll be ready if you let me get up,"

"You got ten minutes," she warned.

Just like normal black folks, late as usual, I heard the horn honking outside about twenty minutes later.

"Skkkyyy!" my mom yelled from downstairs. "They're outside honking for you."

"Tell 'em to come up." I was trying my best to hurry up so I wouldn't have to hear their mouths.

"Damn! Why you not dressed yet?" came from the smart ass in the group, Mashae. Her mouth got us into a lot of drama (fist fights) in the past, but she's been my best friend since middle school, so I learned to deal with it.

"Cause that sexy nigga from last night had me tied up," I said, with a smile.

"Oh! He called you?" she asked, just as excited as I was.

"Yeah, and wanted to take me out to breakfast, but ya'll whores always messing shit up for me." I rolled my eyes as I continued to dress.

"Well, if it's meant it will be."

"I guess if it was meant for you to shut up sometimes you would?"

Kizzy joined the conversation. "Shut up and get dressed," she said, pushing me on the bed.

When we arrived at the King of Prussia mall, it was crowded as usual. It seemed like everybody was getting ready for this party. "What store we hitting first?"

"Let's go to Sax, I heard they're having a sale," Armani suggested, ready to spend. "I need a new D&B bag anyway."

We all found dresses at reasonable prices in a reasonable amount of time. That was a first, but now it was time to find footwear. While walking through the mall, I heard a couple females snickering behind me. I wasn't too sure if they wanted me to hear them, but I didn't even bother to ask.

"Aint that the bitch Key was talking to last night?" one asked the other.

"Hold the fuck…" Armani said, turning around.

5

I cut her short to handle it myself, turned around and said, "Yeah, and I'm the bitch that's gonna be fuck'n him tonight."

They were stunned. I don't know if it was because I heard them or because I had the nerve to answer the question. What I do know is they aint have nothing else to say, so we kept it moving. We weren't about to be fighting so their corny asses could fuck up our hair anyway.

We got out the mall at approximately two-thirty and went straight to South Philly Nails to do the manicure and pedicure thing. A girl's day out is what it turned in to be.

When I finally got home, I tried to get some rest before the party. It was Q, one of Armani's brothers, album release party being hosted by Golden Girl from Power 99 FM. He's been in the industry for years, so anybody who was somebody was going to be there. I knew there would be drama for sure. That was the thing in the hood. It seemed like large crowds just called out for violence. If people would act as if they had some real sense, maybe we would be more liable to enjoy ourselves for once. The phone rang bringing me from my nod.

"Are you getting ready girl?" It was Kizzy knowing damn well I wasn't dressed.

"What time is it?" I yawned into the phone.

"Ten o'clock. Don't start that yawning shit in my ear. Get up!"

"Damn, I didn't know I was sleep that long. I'm getting up now."

"We'll be over there in about an hour." She sounded very anxious. I don't know why because with her psycho baby father there, it wasn't like she could do anything.

I rolled out the bed and went to hop in the shower. While ironing my clothes, my mom came into the room with a concerned look.

"Skyy, I need you to do something for me."

"What's up, Mom?"

"I need you to talk to Samir," she paused. "Something has been bothering him lately and he won't talk to me. He opens up to you more."

"I'll talk to him, Mom. I'm sure everything is okay."

Samir is my 17-year-old brother. The majority of his issues have to do with females. I told him once before, he falls too easily. Being as though this would be his last year in high school, I told him to breathe easy. When he gets to college he'll have a lot of time to fall in love.

"Have fun tonight baby and be careful," she said, giving me a kiss.

"Okay, Mom. I love you."

By the time we arrived at the club, it was so much traffic the lines swung around the corner. I was glad we didn't have to stand in them. Of course we were on the guest list for the VIP section. The crowd inside and out was thick like Memorial Day weekend in Miami. Females were dressed in skin tight clothing with nothing but ass cheeks and titties showing. Some men were doing the grown up thing dressed in slacks and shoes, while others thuged it out in street wear. 7th & Spring Garden was definitely looking like Greek weekend that night.

As we entered, all I could think about was what the highlight of the night would be. It was jam packed shoulder to shoulder. The dance floor was off the chain. I'm use to seeing everybody standing around thinking they're too cute to dance, but not tonight. While making our way through the crowd, my focus was temporarily snatched by GG up on stage doing her thang. She was dressed to impress rocking pink from head to toe and making her trademark name, *The Black Barbie*, a proven fact. Still squeezing through available openings in the crowd, I couldn't help but stare in silence at the familiar face in front of me.

I finally snapped out my trance. "How you been, Slim?" I asked, with a devilish grin.

He looked me up and down. "Chillin' babe. What's been up wit you?"

"Hanging in there. Gettin' ready to go away to school."

I wanted him to know that after all he'd put me through, I didn't give up and I didn't let him destroy my self-esteem like he had set out to do. *"You need me cause aint nobody else gon want you all used up"* is what he use to say.

"That's wassup. Stay focused."

I could tell in his voice he was angry, so I had to rub it in some more. "Oh I am. Trust me," I emphasized every word in slow motion. The look he gave me was crazy. He was hatin' and I loved it, every bit.

"Maybe we can go out one day. You know, to catch up on old times."

"Maybe not," I replied, coming closer to whisper in his ear. "Remember, I'm focused now."

"You tryna play me like a nut?"

"No, I'm keeping it real. You know that's what I do," I grinned, attempting to walk away. "I'll see you around."

"Just to let you know, you wearing the shit out that dress," he yelled, with his words being drowned out by the music.

"Thank you. I'll take that as a compliment even though I know you're tryna win points."

"You know I aint never gonna change."

"That's why I'm a keep it moving. I holla." I winked and walked away.

When I reached the VIP section, the girls had already found us a few seats. The first face I noticed sitting across in another section of VIP made my heart skip a beat. It was Key, looking sexier than Jordan in his Hanes underwear, with a female up in his face. He didn't see me yet, so I played it cool and went to sit down.

"Aint that ya boy over there?" asked Mashae, noticing as well.

"Yup, that's him. Stop looking so hard," I said, smacking her. "Turn around."

"You might as well stop tripping cause he's about to come over here."

My heart was pounding and my stomach had butterflies.

"Oh! He's going down the steps. You can breathe now."

"Skyy, I haven't seen you like this over somebody in a while. What's the deal?" Kizzy asked, examining my expression.

I never took my eyes off Key as he made his way through the crowd. "What are you talking about?"

"Nothing since you wanna play dumb."

"Whatever Kizzy!"

"That seems to be your favorite line when something true flies your way," she commented, referring to the word *whatever*.

I did use that a lot when hiding from the truth. All of them burst into laughter. I guess I made it real noticeable how this guy had me feeling. The last person I felt this way about was Slim, and he damn near killed my ass, so maybe it was time to slow my role.

I laughed with them. "Oh, it's funny, huh?"

"Yeah, cause it's the truth," said Mashae, still laughing.

"You just know everything. Why am I acting like this?"

"Because you need some dick." She spelled it out for me. "D.I.C.K."

Everybody high-fived. It's been about a good year since I had some. After I left Slim alone and he went to prison, I never really gave anyone else the time of day. Maybe she was right. A little sex always seemed to make my mood more pleasurable, and I was a bit tired of my finger. I started to thrive just thinking about it.

"That was a cute suggestion," I giggled.

Armani headed toward the steps. "Time to get drunk. I'm going to the bar."

I hopped up to follow. "Wait! I'm going with you."

"Bring us back something."

"If somebody buys my drink I'm not bringing back shit," I assured them.

When I hit the bottom of the stairwell, I felt a hand touch mine. It was Key and I was stuck for words. "What's up pretty lady? You're fitting that dress," he remarked.

All I could do was smile. The boy had me acting stuck on stupid. Now I was sure no one ever had me tripping like this before. This was serious.

He continued. "Where you going?"

"To get a drink."

"Let me walk you." He grabbed my hand. "Can't let nobody snatch you up."

"I got this big daddy. I'm a big girl. Can't you tell?" I smiled and walked away giving him the look of life. I could feel his eyes rolling up and down every inch of my body.

Armani passed me an apple martini when I reached the bar. "I needed this," I said, taking a gulp.

"I saw you talking to Key. What did he say?"

"Let's just say I got to play my part with this cat and get my act together."

"You right. Don't be giving in all easy. You know he's a *beast* about to be making it big."

We both took a drink on that one and headed out to the dance floor. Q got on the mic and thanked everyone for coming out and dedicated the night to his homie who was gunned down a week ago. There was a moment of silence, then the DJ played my song and it was curtains.

Everybody heard it was *Back That Ass Up* by Juvenile and went crazy. Kizzy and Mashae came down on the floor to join us. I felt someone come behind me to dance, but didn't turn around. From the look on Armani's face, I knew it had to be somebody I wanted there so I kept doing my thing. When I realized it was Key, my panties got wet. He was giving me one of those seductive looks like I was supposed to read his mine. If he was thinking what I was thinking, we both were ready to break fast and get a room. As bad as I wanted to, I ignored the temptation.

POWPOWPOWPOW...Gunshots rang out and everyone started ducking. People were tumbling over chairs desperate for an escape.

11

"I knew this shit was gon happen." I grabbed Kizzy and Armani. "Where is Mashae?"

"There she is. Grab her." Kizzy said, spotting her.

We spotted Q by the DJ booth and ran over to where he stood. He ordered us to stay put and don't move from that spot until he got back.

"Why can't niggas act right? Messed my whole night up!" whined Mashae.

"Just be quiet Mashae. I just hope aint nobody dead."

Just then we heard somebody yell, "Oh shit! Chuck got hit!" Instantly, we all stood up and headed to the front door. Chuck is Q's right hand man.

The pitch of Armani's high voice kept screeching, "Where is my brother?" All I could do was try to keep her calm, but it wasn't working. "No! Where the fuck is my brother?" she repeated.

When we made our way to out the front entrance and down the small flight of cemented stairs, Q was kneeling over Chuck who was stretched out on the pavement beside his car. "Somebody call an ambulance" voices screamed out, and then more shots filled the air. People were trampling over the railing just above where we stood. Others were diving to the ground for safety. A full blown stampede was going on.

What the hell is going on? I thought, watching everyone scatter.

By the time Armani crawled to Q, he was stretched out over Chuck. "NO! NO! NO! NO! NO!"

It took the cops about ten minutes to get there and the ambulance an extra five. They tried to get reports from whomever they could.

12

We left the scene to head to the hospital. When we called our parents to let them know what happened, everyone came down to the Emergency Room. My Aunt Tee, Armani and Q's mother, flipped out soon as she came through the automatic glass doors. "Where is my boy?" she repeated over and over.

Armani held her mom trying to keep her calm. "Mommy, it's okay. He's gon be okay. He's gotta be okay."

It was nothing but chaos in the waiting room. All we could do was cry and pray until the doctor came out to tell us the status. When that time came, it was about six-forty in the morning. As the doctor approached us, he said both surgeries went well and that both Chuck and Q were in stable condition. Our mourns turned into tears of joy. We all were happy to hear the good news. Some family decided to stick around, but us girls headed to Armani's house to get some rest. Around noon, Armani headed back up to the hospital, while the rest of us went home.

I noticed the red light on my answering machine blinking when I reached my bedroom door. The phone was also ringing, so I went for that instead.

"Hey, are you alright?" asked Key, worried.

"Yeah, I'm cool. Thanks for calling, but I'm about to lay down for a minute."

"I can dig it. Just wanted to check on you. Call me when you get a chance. I'll be chilling down at the Plat."

The Plateau is the hang out spot on Sundays in Fairmont Park where people went to flirt, chill, drink, smoke weed, etc...

"Will do," I said hanging up with a smile.

I passed out before remembering to click the button for the messages.

•• *Key* ••

Meanwhile, on the other side of town, I was hanging out with my right hand man, Rome. As we passed a blunt back and forth, I leaned on my motorcycle and checked out the scenery. The Plat was crowded, but that was usual for a Sunday. Females would throw on their skimpiest outfits and the fellas would throw on their tightest gear thinking they looked better and better every weekend. Horns were honking and the beat of *Yeah That's Us* boomed out of car stereos as traffic was tied up bumper to bumper.

"Was that your Shorty?" asked Rome.

I giggled imagining how Skyy was backing that ass up on me last night. "Yeah, that was her."

"She was looking real lovely last night. I bet she taste good too."

"I'll find out soon enough if she stops teasing me," I replied, hoping she would give in sooner than later.

"You know these females got to play hard to get."

"I know!" I smirked at the females walking back and forth trying to get my attention. "She doesn't think I know the rules of the game."

"You about to be getting a couple dollars, so she has to front like she aint interested."

"I'll get her. That's my goal."

"When you do, smack that ass for me." Rome portrayed as if he was smacking someone on the ass from behind.

"You stupid. Let me hit that L, dawg." I took a couple puffs wondering how long it would be before Skyy gave in.

"Damn! Look at shorty right there with that fat ass," exclaimed Rome, gesturing for a couple of females to come over there. "Ay Sis, come here for a minute."

"Don't call them groupies over here."

"Man, look at the ass on that chick."

All I could do was laugh. When they came over, I didn't acknowledge either of the two females.

"What's up, Ma?" Rome asked the taller one of the girls.

"Nothing Pa. Is that how you greet people?" she asked.

"No, but that's how I greeted you."

Both girls introduced themselves as Jae, who was more of a thin caramel complexion, averaging at about 5'7, with a short haircut. The other was NeNe. She was short and firm, like a Jada Pinkett/Nia Long type female. She too had a short haircut, and was taking much interest into me.

She looked over and said, "Hi friend."

I responded in an arrogant tone, "Wassup?"

"Damn, somebody pissed you off or is your tongue too tight?" she joked, not too enthused by his response.

I had to scope her from top to bottom cause she was fine as hell. "I'm cool, Ms. NeNe. Where ya'll headed? Maybe we can go."

"Maybe not," NeNe said, never loosing that smile.

Rome gave me a pound and said, "We got us a comedian. Let's roll out and go get something to eat."

"Sounds like a plan," Jae advised. "We'll meet ya'll down on 52nd so we can park the car and hop on the bikes."

"That's a bet. Come on Key, let's be out," Rome agreed by starting his engine and we were off.

Chapter 2

MEN

Ry the time I got up to get in the shower, it was hitting five on the nose. When I got back to my bedroom, I finally decided to check my missed messages. I flopped diagonally across the bed still wrapped in my towel and reached over to hit the play button. Three were from people asking if I was okay, one was a hang up, and the last was from Slim. The message sent a chill through my body. I listened to it twice not quite understanding the point of it, but got a bad vibe. I saved it and got dressed.

The house was empty, so I headed right out the door. When I got to my car, there was a note on the windshield. It read: *Call me ASAP 215-555-1254 Slim!* I began to think about the message as I drove away.

My destination was Kizzy's house to see what she was up to. She and Mashae were on the sofa eating and watching TV, so I made a plate and joined them.

"Did ya'll talk to Armani?" I asked, concerned. I knew better than anybody how personal she takes her brother because I'm the same way about mines. Samir is one person I'd definitely loose control over.

"No, her cell phone is off."

"Let's go down to the hospital to see what's up."

"Everything is cool," Mashae said, getting up to take her plate in the kitchen. "Kizzy called down there and talked to your mom. She said Q is starting to respond."

I was relieved to hear he was doing okay. "Thank God!"

"I can't believe this shit happened." Kizzy was aggravated and upset. "I knew it was gonna be some jerks to mess up the party."

"I'm just glad everything is cool. It could have been a lot worse."

"Yeah, you right. Did you talk to Key?"

At the mention of his name, I could feel my insides thrive. I don't know what it is about him, but whatever it is was driving me crazy. Just the thought of him made me tingle. Come on, now how many guys you know are capable of doing that? Especially one you never been intimate with!

"He called earlier and said he was down at the Plat."

"It's probably poppin' down there right now. Come on, let's take a ride."

She didn't have to say it twice because I got up ready to go with Mashae right behind me.

As we rode through 52nd street, it was loud and the traffic was ridiculous. People were honking horns, hollering back and forth across the street, and running around acting stupid. I heard someone yelling my name. When I turned around, it was Jae and NeNe approaching on foot.

"Where ya'll been? NeNe I aint seen you in a month of Sundays?" I asked, wondering why I haven't seen them since graduation.

"I was tied down." She filled us in on her up-to-date relationship with her college man. He was very aggressive and insecure. It was always hard to get her to go out with us on the weekends when we were in school.

I gave an astonished look. "So what? He let you out?"

"He left to go attend a medical seminar for school."

Mashae leaned over sticking her head out the driver side window. "Where ya'll going, Jae?"

"We just got off the motorcycles with these guys that took us to get something to eat."

"I feel like getting on a bike right now," I advised.

Most people had freaky fetishes, but not me. My fetish was to ride. There was nothing I enjoyed more than flying in the wind down the expressway on the back of a Kawasaki 900. Slim started to teach me how to ride before he got locked up, but I be damned if I asked to continue where we'd left off.

"I heard what happened last night. Is everything cool?" NeNe asked, concerned about the shooting. News flew around the hood even before the media could get a leak.

"They're gonna be alright. Thank God." I looked up to thank him once again.

"Niggas always got to act up."

"You know it. Jealousy gets you nowhere."

"Ya'll going to the club tonight?"

"I doubt it. I had enough action for one weekend."

"I know that's right. Well, I'll holla at ya'll later cause aint nothing going on out here," she said, heading back towards her car.

"So what's next troops?" I asked, getting back in to join Mashae and Kizzy.

"Take me home so I can find somebody to lay up with," Mashae said.

That was Mashae for you. So blunt and out spoken about sex, or should I just say dick. I guess that was the one thing that motivated her, besides her daughter, of course. She was 5'4, light skin and quick tempered. Her lightweight was a deceiving means for a strong woman. She also had a smile for days that would seize any guy to her needs. I asked her time and time again why she doesn't make amends with her daughter's father, but she's too damn stubborn to even listen. He really pissed her off by cheating. I told her it comes with the game.

"Mashae, is that all you know how to do?"

"Yup, you know it," she said, meaning every word.

I just shook my head. "Kizzy, where you going?"

"Take me to my mom's house so I can get my kids."

Kizzy had a 5-year-old boy, and a 2-year-old girl by her mate of seven years, Tyrik. She too was a beauty out our click. Her frame was also 5'4 and the thickest of us all. The complexion she obtained was between a bronze and caramel looking as if she were mixed. Truth be told, she was all sistah and flaunted it well. Her situation was a little different, but still going through the bullshit just like any other female. And speaking of the devil, there stood Tyrik posted up on 52nd Street.

"Aint that Tyrik over there?" Mashae asked, spotting him.

"Yes, it is," Kizzy confirmed, trying to open the door while I was still driving. "Let me out this muthafucking car."

"Hold up, Kizzy." I tried to slow down before she killed herself. "Let me park."

"No, let me out. Did he see you, Mashae?" she asked, hoping he didn't so she could creep up and catch him in action.

"I don't think so."

Can't have one day of peace, I quietly thought. After getting a good look at the girl he was with, I recalled her being the same chick Kizzy had problems with in the past. "That's the same girl from last time."

Kizzy tied her hair in a ponytail and jumped out of the car. "I'm a whip this bitch ass. Pass me my mace!" She headed straight towards them. "Tyrik, you really think I'm playing with you don't you?"

"Hold up. I'm not even doing nothing," he said, trying to sound sincere.

That didn't help. Kizzy pulled out the can of mace and sprayed him directly in his face damn near emptying the entire bottle. The crowd started moving back from the fumes. "How do that shit feel?" she yelled.

"Why the fuck you mace me? I can't see shit," he said, while taking his shirt off to clear his eyes.

"You aint suppose to, muthafucker! That's the point." She three pieced him and started to spray again until the chick butted in.

"Look, we were just talking," the girl said in a nasty tone. You would've thought she had enough sense to leave by now.

"Didn't I tell you if I saw you in his face again I was gon hurt you?" Kizzy grabbed her as she tried to take off running. "Don't run." She threw two punches and the girl swung back catching Kizzy in the chin. "Oh you want to swing back." Kizzy tossed her on the ground trying to stomp a mud hole in her.

We stood back making sure none of her nut ass friends tried anything, which they didn't. That couldn't have been me getting my ass kicked and my girls didn't help. That's another rule in the book. The hell with a fair one if I'm getting my ass whipped.

"Won't ya'll stop her before she kills that girl?" Tyrik said since no one else bothered to stop it. That's just how nosy people are in the hood.

"Won't you mind your business? Whip her ass Kizzy!" I said, cheering her on.

Kizzy was dragging her from the sidewalk to the street. I didn't bother to ask where the hell she was going because when she blacks out like that, it isn't anything anybody could say to her.

When the sirens became an ear full, that's when I got worried. We all got locked up a couple months ago for the same thing except it was Mashae with the drama. "Here comes them boys!" someone yelled out the crowd.

"Get your girl before she gets locked up again," Tyrik demanded, never attempting to get her himself.

"Come on, Kizzy."

"No, I'm a kill her! Every time I see you I'm a whip your ass just for GP. Every Time!" Kizzy barked, stressing her intentions.

Mashae already had jumped in the car after getting flashbacks of that jail cell she sat in for 48 hours. "Come on Kizzy. I don't feel like this jail shit again. Grab her, Skyy."

Kizzy tried to go after Tyrik. "Don't come home tonight cause your shit won't be there."

"Girl, get in the car and shut up."

When we pulled off, I could see the fire in her eyes expressing the anger. "I'm so fucking heated right now. I don't believe he still messing with her."

"You know she don't give a shit about you and he just following the pussy. Fuck him girl, especially with all these niggas that been on you lately. Stop playing around and play your part. That's what he doing." Mashae suggested, being a bit cruel.

I, on the other hand, was tired of going through this with her, but even more tired of Tyrik. "Dammit Kizzy, stop crying! Aren't you tired of crying? You should be out of tears by now."

"I know, but this shit hurts." She tried to hold the tears back but they kept coming like an ongoing faucet. "I don't do nothing but try to be what he wants me to be and he still don't appreciate nothing I do."

"Well, since you know this, get it together and move on. He's only gonna keep doing what you allow him to do."

The car went silent the rest of the ride home. I sat there thinking about how Slim use to treat me. Kizzy was always there to give me advice, but what was so hard that she couldn't take her own. I guess it's true when they say sometimes you can help another better than you can help yourself.

After the drop off, I headed back home to rest my mind. I cut my ringer and cell phone off so I could take a minute out for myself. There was so much going on around me. The meditation wasn't that easy because too much weighed on my mind, especially that message from Slim. I couldn't grasp the point of it or the vibe it gave me. He always got some shit with him. That was one thing I was sure of, but what was it this time?

23

Chapter 3

CAN'T LIVE WITH THEM

I t's been about two weeks and everybody was getting ready for the big July 4th block party. Key and I went out a few times, but I was still playing my part. Kizzy had finally decided to let Tyrik come home after all his begging and pleading. Q and Chuck were home from the hospital taking it easy. Rumors said that whoever was the reason behind their situation wouldn't be a reason for long.

The neighborhood guys ran around squirting people with super soakers, and whoever walked by thinking they were hot stuff got drenched, even strangers. The smell of barbequed ribs and macaroni & cheese smothered our noses as we all gathered around laughing and joking having a good ol' time.

"Hey Skyy, where you been?" asked Aunt Tee.

She was more like a mother figure to everyone. Most people called her Mom Tee being the mother hen of the hood. To know her was to love her, but you had to know when and where to draw the line. Everyone has that one family member that don't take *no* shit, and sure enough, she was the one in my family.

"I've been chilling, Auntie. Staying out of trouble."

"You better cause your ass is out of here come September." She gave me the look like if you're not I'm going to kick your butt.

"I know it's time to get out of here and do the college thing." I saw Armani heading to the car so I used her as an escape goat to get out of dodge before getting the big lecture. "Where you going, Armani?"

"To the store. Ride with me, Kizzy." She nodded toward a car that was parking. "I'm not even gonna ask you cause look who just pulled up."

It was Key, pulling up in his jet black JAG with the butter black leather interior. The car was ridiculously clean. It matched just right with his silky soft complexion. His tall frame and miraculous build reminded me of a darker version of Tyson Beckford (the model), and his face was shaved to perfection giving a baby face appearance.

I kept my eyes on him as he stepped out the car thinking how he'd handle all the groupies tonight. It was just a matter of time before one tried to be all in his face, so I sat back in the cut and watched him play it out.

"Hey Key," one of the fellas said, giving a handshake. "What's up wit Miami? That's who ya rolling wit right?"

"Yeah, that's where I'll be." He noticed one of his old flames approaching fast. "Here comes this dizzy ass broad. Is Skyy over there?" He began to scan the crowd.

I watched from a distance. He couldn't see me, but I could sure see him.

"Hey Tykey. Where you been lookin' all good?" she asked, licking her lips.

"Why you shouting out my whole MO like that?"

"That's how you use to like it. What changed?"

"Me and You, so keep stepping." He tried to walk away but she stood in front of him.

"I know you aint tryna front cause that bitch over there. I heard ya'll creepin'." She turned around to see if I was watching the show, which I was, but she couldn't see me either.

He frowned with disgust. "What are you talking about? Aint nobody creepin'."

"Nigga please. She aint got nothing on me, so what's the deal?"

"If you don't get out my ear talking this bull, I'm a slap the shit out you."

"You know I like it rough. What, you forgot?"

He pushed her back. "Get the fuck out ma face."

"Yo Key, take a walk before Skyy come over here and the party be shut down," his homie Kenny warned him.

"Let that bitch come over here. What she gon do to me?" the chick tempted feeling offended.

"Sis, I think you better roll cause you in the wrong place to be talking shit. These are her peoples. Not yours!" Kenny warned her this time.

"Fuck you, Tykey. You aint shit and aint never gon be shit with your conceited ass. She'll find out soon enough." She walked away switching back and forth, hoping he would follow, but felt stupid cause he didn't.

Aunt Tee walked over to see what was going on. "What's the problem fellas?"

"Nothing, Mom Tee. Everything is everything," Kenny quickly responded.

"I'm talking to Mr. Tykey. Why that heffa walking away like something stuck up her ass?" she questioned, but didn't give him a chance to answer. "Don't get my niece caught up in your bull shit cause I'll be the one on your ass."

26

"These females be acting crazy," he responded, knowing that wasn't a good enough answer. It was the best thing he could come up with at the time.

"Stop fucking them all crazy and they might act sane." She popped him upside the head with a serious look.

He just laughed and said, "You crazy."

"It's not funny and I'm not joking. I don't want to have to kill nobody."

I finally came over to be nosy and find out what was going on not looking Key's way. "Aunt Tee, where is the rest of the meat?"

"Hello to you too, Skyy."

"I'll holla at you later," I frowned.

"Somebody in trouble," Kenny chuckled.

"Shut up, Kenny." He grabbed my arm as I went to walk away. "Wait! Let me holla at you for a minute. I'm trying to go to AC tonight. You wanna go?"

As bad as I wanted to say yeah, I couldn't sound pressed. "I might. I'll let you know."

"Make it soon cause if you go we gon stay over."

I grinned and walked away heading for Armani's car that had just returned. "Ya'll took long enough just to be getting bread."

"We had to make it ourselves," Armani said, being sarcastic.

"Okay, smart ass. That's why J.J came by here looking for you."

"For real? Stop playing."

J.J was her first and last love. Ever since he'd left town on her without a word, she decided not to trust another man considering them all jokes in her eyes.

"I'm serious. I told him you be right back but you took too long." Just as I was telling her, my Aunt Tee yelled across the street and confirmed it. "Told you I wasn't lying, tramp."

"Damn!" she stomped away. "I missed my boy. Watch he don't come back."

Now Armani was the tallest of us all. She was 5'8 with long black hair, which she kept braided up. Her styles mimicked the styles of Alicia Keys every time she got a chance. But the thing that stood out the most was her big beautiful brown eyes and clean shaved long legs. I told her time and time again her money needs to be made modeling. She just laughs it off.

The time was quickly passing and the sun had gone down. The outside lamp lightened the card table as we sat playing Spades.

"Key wants me to go to AC with him tonight," I advised, to see what kind of feedback I would get.

"Are you going?"

"Maybe." I still wasn't too sure if I should or not. I knew if I did, there would be a ninety percent chance that he was getting some.

"Stop frontin' on the brotha. I heard he got a big one," conveyed Mashae.

"All you think about is dick, Mashae. Is that why your mouth so big?"

"Don't hate. I don't have a man so I'm free to do what I want."

"I'm a find you one so you can slow your ass down." I began to plead my case about being indecisive. "If I give him some, he aint going to know how to act. Ya'll know how these niggas be trippin'."

"Let him trip and stick ya hands right in them pockets."

They all agreed by giving a high five.

"The nigga might make me trip. Then what? I'm not tryna get hurt again."

Every time I thought about a new relationship, it frustrated me. My last relationship with Slim and all the things he put me through made it hard to move on. All the lies, bruises and females I caught him with were enough. But they say what goes around comes around. I use to be the one doing the dirt. Now that I know what it feels like, I wouldn't ever do it to anyone again.

"Don't put your heart in it. Just let nature take its course."

"Listen to you, Armani. You know how I feel after the sex thing, especially if I'm feeling the dude."

"I know, and that's what you need to work on."

"Aint nothing to work on. I can't control feelings I have for somebody. I'm not as hard as you."

That was one thing I loved about Armani. She was a true pimp when it came to males. Always had them eating out the palms of her hands. Some females just had that affect on men.

"You don't need to be having sex then cause you been done got hurt five more times."

"Fuck it! I'm going. Aint nothing else to do."

Kizzy butted in. "Who knows? This might be the *one*."

"Shut up!" the three of us said at the same time.

"I'm about to shoot home and get an overnight bag. I'll be back."

I headed to my car trying to locate Key, but he wasn't anywhere in sight. That was because he was on my heels trying to find out where I was going. He blocked me from opening my car door with a questionable look.

"I'm going home for a second. I'll be right back."

"What's the verdict? Are you going or not?" he asked sounding pressed, but I didn't want to play him.

"I guess so. I'm not doing anything else."

"I'll see you when you get back. I'm gonna make a run so just call my cell phone when you're ready."

I got in the car watching his sexy bow legged ass walk away. He knew he was the shit and couldn't nobody tell him different.

Why he got to be so sexy? I asked myself as I drove away fantasizing about us in the hotel room. *I got to put my thing down on this nigga. I just got to or I might as well forget it.*

•• *Key* ••

While sitting on the hood of my car, I couldn't help but think of my lil fly mama. *I knew she was gonna go talking bout she might have something to do. I got to give it to her though, the chick knows how to make it sound good.* She is definitely worth taking out the hood.

"Yo Kenny, come take a ride with me!" I yelled, to get his attention.

"Hold up a second. I have to do something." Kenny ran around the corner to handle some business.

I propped myself up on the hood of my car waiting patiently for his return. After spotting Armani across the street, I took that time to get in her head a little. "Armani, come here a minute."

She walked over suspiciously wondering what I wanted.

"You know I'm about to take your girl to AC, right?"

"Yeah, she needs to get away."

"What kind of food does she like? I want to have the room and everything set up for her."

Armani was outspoken and blunt just like her mom. If you didn't like what she had to say, oh well. "Don't be tryna score points for some ass," she warned, being hip to my game.

"It aint even about that. I'm feelin' her."

"Please don't be a fuck up cause she's been through enough."

I stared out offensively. "I said I'm feeling her."

"All I'm saying is that she's real, so keep it real with her. If this is about you getting some ass, just let her know what the deal is cause if she wanna give you some she will."

"I'm not tryna play head games wit her. Just answer my question and save the lecture."

"She loves lasagna. That's her favorite dish."

"Aint that some shit? That's my favorite." I gave a soft jab to her chin letting her know she can ease up because I'm not out to dog her girl. "I got her. She's safe with me."

"I'ma hold you to that."

"I meant to tell you, my homie Rome asks about you all the time. The one I was wit at *Chrome*."

"He was a cutie. Give him my number," she blushed.

31

Kenny jogged back around the corner cutting our conversation. "You ready, Key?"

"I'll give it to him for you," I said, hopping down from the hood. I left smiling from ear to ear knowing tonight was gonna be my night to taste the sweetness.

•• *Skyy* ••

When I pulled up to my house, I noticed an unfamiliar car parked on the other side of the street, but there wasn't anyone in it. As I reached into my pocketbook for my house keys, someone ran up behind me and covered my mouth.

He whispered in my ear, "I thought you were focused." Instantly, I knew who it was. Slim!

He turned me around and said, "I miss you."

"Slim, let me go. What's the matter with you scaring me like that?"

"You told me you are focused. I was making sure, but I see you're not."

"Why are you out here in the dark?" I asked, hoping he wasn't stalking me.

"I was waiting for you."

My nerves were shot. "For what? What do you want?"

"I saw you at the cookout earlier. Had to tell you how good you looked."

"Thank you!" I tried to make my way to my house.

He put his arm out to block. "I waited for you all this time and you gon play me? Nah, that's not how you do me." He grabbed me closer to him.

32

"I'm not playin' you. They are waiting for me to come back. Why are you holding me so tight?" I tried to loosen his grip.

"I miss you. I miss you a lot." He pulled me closer against the car and tried to kiss me. "How much you miss me?"

I knew damn well he didn't really want me to answer that question. If he did, he was crazy. I was going to tell him just how much I missed him, but decided not to, being in the predicament I was in with no one around.

"Come on Slim, we went through this before. Didn't we both agree to let each other go and move on?"

"No, you agreed to let me go and move on." He tried to kiss me again but I continued to turn away.

"Please don't do this," I begged.

"I still love you, Skyy. You'll always be mines." He loosened up a bit to look me in the eye. "I left my number on your car. Why you aint call me yet?"

"I've been busy," I lied. I had let the number fly out the window while driving down the street.

"Oh, I see now. You're too busy for me. Busy with who?"

The look in his eyes made me very uncomfortable. It was the same look I use to get before he would beat on me.

"Nobody. I've been going through a lot. I need some *Me* time." I tried to calm him down and get his mind off of me being with someone else.

"I gave you *Me* time. Now it's *Our* time," he implied, with a serious tone.

"I told you, I'm done. There's no more *Us*."

"You think? There will always be an *Us*. Nobody else can have you." He gave me the same scary look again. "Don't make me kill nobody."

33

Why did it feel like he meant what he said. "You need to get it together Slim, fast! Let me go so I can handle my business."

As I turned and walked away he said, "I'll see you again. Just remember what I said on that message."

What is up with that message? What does it mean? When I turned around to ask him, he sped off in a dark-blue Buick with tinted windows and the music blasting. I let the thought go and went inside. Samir was on the sofa watching TV, so I took the time to talk to him.

"What's up knucklehead? Where is Mommy?" I asked, plopping down on the sofa.

"She's down the street," he answered, still flicking through the channels.

I was wondering what could be bothering him that much to keep him in on the 4th of July. "Why you in the house?"

He responded with silence.

I reached over to cut the TV off. "Oh boy, what's up?"

"I'm staying in here cause if I go outside I might hurt somebody."

"What she do now?" I asked, assuming he was referring to a female.

"I don't know what's the matter with that girl."

"Which one?"

"All of 'em crazy." He threw his hands up in the air. "She sliced my tires again."

"If you stop thinking you're a pimp, maybe you'll be able to keep a car for a whole month."

"Why is that the first thing these chicks go after?"

"Because they know how much you love your cars. I'm gonna let you know now, I'm tired of whipping their asses for you when I know you're wrong."

"Better you than me cause I been done went to jail."

"It's sad cause if it was me, I would do the same thing to ya black ass." I mugged him.

"I can't help it if my stroke game is off the wall. Blame it on Daddy."

"Whatever nigga. Get your mind right. When these niggas try to do me dirty, you be ready to kill somebody."

"So what, that's different," he explained, but there was no difference.

Men need to learn to treat a female the same way they want their mom, sisters, aunts, or any other female they care about treated. As soon as someone does to them the same thing that goes on out in the streets, they be ready to snap.

"It's not different, Samir. It will come back on you." I stood up. "You know better than anyone else how I use to be with guys. Having them loving me to death and dog them for whatever I can. Soon as I got good and in love, all that dirt came back. It hurts baby boy, so you better slow down." I threw the TV remote in his lap.

"I'm a big boy. I can handle mines," he jokingly responded.

"Don't say I aint warn you Big Dog. Just stay out of trouble before you give Mommy a heart attack, then I'll be on your ass." I headed upstairs.

"After all these years you still think you can beat me."

"I love you silly. Go get some fresh air, and tell Mom I'll be back tomorrow."

I packed a little bag and headed back to the block.

•• *Key* ••

On the other side of town, Kenny and I took a trip to my girlfriend's house. A girlfriend Skyy had no idea about, but can't say she wasn't sure I had one. Who wouldn't want this tall, sexy brother looking as good as I did? She probably thinks I have three or four girls. I'll be her boy toy for the night so that's all that matters.

I pulled out my phone when I arrived outside the door. "Latasha, come to the door."

"Who is this?" she questioned being spiteful, but I was in no mood for games. "I thought we were going to AC," she babbled.

"Man, come to the door before I leave."

I started the engine and she flew to the door to let us inside. "What's up, Kenny?" she said, rolling her eyes at me. "I'm tired of your bullshit, Tykey."

"What you talking 'bout now?"

"I been in here all day waiting for you to come and get me."

"My bad baby, I been running all day. That's what I came to explain." I pushed her against the wall and kissed her.

She pushed me off. "Whatever Key, you could have called."

"I promise I'll make it up tomorrow, okay?" I went to walk toward the door to get her attention.

She ran behind me like I knew she would. "It's not too late. Why can't we still go?"

"Because I ain't finish. I still got other shit to do."

"Or somebody to do!?!" she spat raising her voice.

A novel by Nyema

That was my cue. I stopped and turned around. "Baby, calm down. Why you always have to think it's somebody else?"

"It don't matter cause if it is and I find out, it's not gonna be pretty."

"See what I mean, that's why I don't come in here cause I got to hear your mouth time and time again. Damn! Can't go one day without arguing over something I aint even doing." I walked away still snappin' and she bought every word of it.

"I'm sorry baby. All I'm saying is that I want to spend more time with you."

"Well, stop bitchin' all the time and we will spend more time together. Now come over here and tell me you love me." The reverse psychology works every time.

She walked over obeying my command. "I love you."

"You love who?"

"I love you, Big Daddy."

I smacked her on the ass how she likes it. "I'll call you in a little while when things slow down a bit."

My phone rang revealing Skyy's name. Tasha moved a little closer trying to catch the voice on the other end like I aint know she was tryna be slick. I answered anyway not about to pass up that opportunity. "Wassup?"

"What's up babe? I'm back on the block."

"A'ight. I'll be right there in about 15 minutes."

"If I'm not here, call my cell."

That made me concerned. "Where you going?"

"I might make a run with the girls."

"Stay there. I'll be right..."

Tasha's voice suddenly overpowered mine. "Who the fuck…" she began to question, but the smack to her mouth mid-sentence shut her ass up.

"I'm on my way." I hung up to deal with her.

"Nigga, I'm tired of you putting your hands on me," she cried holding her face in tears.

"You talk too much."

"You talking to a bitch on the phone in my house and gon tell me I talk too much?"

"What the fuck is the matter with you? That was business and you was about to fuck it up."

"That was a bitch. I know how you sound when you're talking to one."

"Fuck this. I'm out." I grabbed the keys off the table. "I'm not for this crying shit. Come on, Kenny." We walked out the door.

She called my name while running to the door. "I'm sick of you. Fuck you and the money you about to get. You aint shit! Fuck you pussy!"

"You really got issues woman. Get your mind right." I proceeded into the car checking the time on my phone.

"If you leave Key, that's it. I mean…"

ERRRRRRRR…The car sped off, and I didn't look back.

I sat on the porch laughing to myself. I heard the chick in the background gasping for air after that smack. Key might think I'm slow, but I'm far from it. Niggas is crazy. They say you can't live with them, can't live without them.

Armani, Mashae and Kizzy pulled up interrupting my thoughts. "Come on, Skyy," Mashae yelled, from the passenger side of the car.

"Nah, ya'll go ahead. I'm waiting for Key to pick me up."
"He'll call when he's ready."

"I said go ahead."

"Let me find out he told you don't move," Kizzy intervened.

"Shut up, Kizzy."

"Have fun. See ya tomorrow."

"Ya'll be careful, you know Armani had a few drinks."

"Please, you know I'm a rider even when I drink."

"I'll holla at ya'll tomorrow," I grinned.

I too was a better driver when I drink or get drunk. I don't know the math to that one, but it was true. After waiting patiently for about 15 minutes, I saw that same dark-blue Buick ride by that Slim was in earlier.

I know this fool is not about to start up again. Damn, I wish Key hurry up. Just as I was wishing it, Key pulled up. *Thank you Lord,* I mumbled jogging down two steps at a time towards the car.

"I see somebody's ready?" he stated. It was bad cause at this point even his voice turned me on.

"Yeah, I have everything. I'm ready to go."

"What you in a rush for?"

"I'm just ready to roll. I'm tired, let's go."

Deep down inside, I knew Slim was going to turn that corner any second and draw on me like he always does.

Key pulled off and said, "You better get un-tired cause I have a big night planned for you."

I was truly tired of playing mind games with him at that point. It was time to let him know how I felt about the charm he'd been laying on me for the last couple weeks. I could be blunt too.

"Look Key, if fucking is the only thing on your mind, you need to slow down a bit and play ya part right."

"Girl, aint nobody worried about that. Why you always have to think I'm on that note?"

"Cause if you are, keep it real. Either way, if I want to fuck you I will, and if I don't I won't." *Damn, I sound like Armani*, I thought to myself.

"I like you. You're the realist Shorty I found in a long time," he smiled.

"Oh, you found me huh?"

"You sure aint find me. You act like you didn't even notice me at *Chrome*."

Little did he know I was watching him out the corner of my eye when Armani told me who he was.

He grabbed my hand unto his and said, "Shorty, I can tell you feeling me. It's time to loosen up a bit."

I didn't have a snappy come back that time so there was no reply.

"I'm not worried about you wanting me cause I'm in the league."

"It's not even about…" I tried to explain, but he stopped me by placing his index finger softly across my lips.

He shushed me. "Shhh," then came over closer. Our faces were only inches apart and I could smell the scent of spearmint from his tongue. "It doesn't matter cause we're gonna enjoy our night together."

How the hell can he be this smooth? It was killing me inside. The rest of the ride to AC was quiet. He played his R&B CD with everyone on it from the Isley Brothers down to Usher. Just the beat from the music alone was making me horny, and the words didn't make it any better.

I used that time to ask myself where he came from and what tomorrow would bring. After I give up the good loving, would he try to play me? Or being that I really dig this guy, should I just tell him I'm not ready? Damn, why is life so complicated? Why is it that if a female give in too soon she's a *whore*, but niggas can stick their dicks in anything and be considered a playa? We got it hard. All the pain we have to endure through life before finding that one to spend the rest of our days with just isn't fair. Life isn't fair is what they say, but I don't care. I planned to take the night for what it was. Whatever happens, happens, cause you only live once.

Chapter 4

CAN'T LIVE WITHOUT THEM

hen we got to the Taj Mahal in Atlantic City, NJ, the scenery was so beautiful. There were still fireworks in the sky, and the casinos were jam packed. I thought about the last time the girls and I came down and got kicked out for being under age. The only one old enough to gamble at the time was Armani. Kizzy almost got us locked up for cursing out the security guards like we were in the right, knowing damn well we were wrong. For some reason, Atlantic City was like a meditation spot for me. Even though there was a lot of action, it felt peaceful. The only down fall about it was the memories of Slim and I riding over here on his motorcycle, just to get away. It wasn't bad then, so I'll get over it.

"Do you like to gamble, Skyy?"

"No, not really. I love money too much to lose any."

"I wish I thought like that." He pinched my butt. "But that's not what tonight is for. This is your night."

I blushed feeling like a kid in a candy store being with him. This feeling has never came upon me before. "So what you got planned?" I asked curiously.

"You'll see in a minute." He grabbed my hand guiding me inside.

"Hey! Mr. Tyson, I see you made it. Everything is set up just as you asked," a well dressed young man behind the counter advised.

I could tell he was a manager or supervisor judging by his attire. Thoughts really started to roll through my head then. I couldn't wait to find out what he had planned.

"Thanks Mike, I'm sure my girl right here will love it," Key responded, smiling down at me.

I got that tingle again. I knew my panties were soaked.

"I guarantee she will have a wonderful time." He passed over a key and escorted us to the elevators.

"Your girl?" I asked, mocking him.

"You will be one day."

Hopefully, I thought. "I see you're real friendly with management. Come here often?"

"It's not like that. My team use to come here a lot. When I got drafted to the Heat, they gave me a little gathering here, so everybody knows who I am."

"That's what they all say." I pinched his butt in return. "Anyway, what floor we on?"

"The top one," he said arrogantly, like I was supposed to jump in his arms or something, but I played it cool.

"What? You got the Penthouse to impress me?"

"No, I got it cause that's what I'm used to being in."

"Oh yeah," I replied.

This nigga think he's the shit for real. I should tell his ass to take me home right now, I considered. But whom was I kidding? It was too late to front on him now.

When we reached the top floor, the elevators opened. There were candles, rose pedals, and balloons everywhere

43

leading into the suite. "What the hell?" I muttered, not aware I was speaking out loud.

"You like it?" he asked, revealing every pearly white tooth in his mouth.

"It's beautiful. What's all this for?"

"Come on inside. I'm starving," he directed, rubbing his tummy.

As I entered the room, it was lit with all types of scented candles, rose pedals leading to the bed with roses all over it, soft music playing by Luther and a candle light dinner for two. This didn't seem like his type. But looks are deceiving, so therefore I better enjoy it while I can. I definitely knew I was giving in now cause he was playing my shit.

"Why you got this baby making music on?"

"What, Luther?" He turned it up a notch. "Who Luther, that's my ma," he smiled. "Go get comfortable so we can sit and eat."

I went in the bathroom to wash off a little. I wanted to call my girls so bad but my phone was out there in my pocketbook. Why is this happening to me Lord, please let him be a good one. I was getting a tad bit excited. I told myself I'd take it for what it's worth, and I was sitting up there talking about him being the *One*.

"Your food is getting cold," he yelled out from the room.

"I'll be out in a minute!" I finished refreshing with my smell goods. "Dammit! I didn't bring the right sleepwear for tonight." I fiddled through my bag. "If I knew it was going to be like this, I would have brought my Vicky Secret lingerie." All I grabbed was a boy-cut short pajama set. "Well this will have to do. He's not going to do nothing but look at my ass anyway."

When I came out he was sitting on the bed looking at me. He gestured for me to come closer. "Damn, you look good. Come here, so I can get a hug."

As he stood up to hug me, he gently started to kiss on my neck and around to my lips. That's when I felt it. Mashae had heard right. It was a big one compared to any I had in the past.

What I don got myself into? I had to think of a way to stop him and get my nerves together.

"Come on Key, let's go eat." I pulled him over to the table. "So what do we have here?" I lift the lid and was surprised. "How'd you know I love lasagna?"

"Cause I love it too," he smiled while stuffing his face at the same time.

We sat eating and passing jokes back and forth. I wasn't fully focused on jokes. My mind was trying to figure out a way to take that big lump in his pants. *Maybe if I just think of how bad I want him to be all mines, I'll be able to take it.* It was definitely time to get drunk.

"Can I have some more wine?"

"You tryna get drunk on me?"

I allowed another lie roll off my tongue. "I don't get drunk."

"Here, drink it all up then." He passed me the whole bottle.

I had about five or six more glasses by the time we were done eating. I grinned from ear to ear feeling the numbness of my bottom lip as the liquor kicked in. That's how I usually could tell when I was about to act a fool.

"Why are you staring at me like that?"

"Cause I can't wait to taste you."

My heart skipped two beats. I could not believe he just said that. "Taste me?" I repeated nonchalantly.

"Yeah, I know you taste good," he assumed, making his lips look wet and juicy. He knew exactly what he was doing.

"I can show you better than I can tell you."

I knew I was drunk when that statement hit the air. I was hardly ready for the pain that I would soon endure. My mouth done got me in trouble once again.

He got up and walked over to me, stood me up and started to kiss all over me. It felt so good I had no choice but to jump into his arms and wrap my legs around his waist. He then walked over to the bed embracing my body like it was a feather in his pocket. He placed me down sucking my breasts, and licking from my belly down my thighs, and to my toes. It was driving me insane.

I sobbed out in a low tone, "Why you keep teasing me? Please stop teasing me."

"You want me to eat it don't you? Tell me how bad you want it," he enticed, seducing my every move.

"I want it, please. I want it! Please don't tease me." He licked every inch of my pussy like he was making love to it. "Oh, I'm 'bout to cum." I was trembling all over.

He muttered while still eating, "Come in my mouth."

And there it was. I came in about 5.4 seconds. That shit never happened to me before in my life. He stayed down there for more than an hour giving me feelings I never knew I had. My orgasm count was up to 6 before I quit keeping up.

He slowly climbed on top of me and whispered in my ear, "You ready for me?"

"Yes, I'm ready," I replied thinking twice. In the back of my mind I was scared to death.

He continued to kiss all over my stomach and my breast inching his way around my neck. We started to kiss passionately as he gently stuck it in. I slid back a little like a punk.

"Don't run, baby. I won't hurt you," he said, trying to make me feel secure.

I got in the groove of it while making all these funny sounds to cope with the pain. I had to find a way to get use to it, and when I did it was on.

"Yeah, that's it baby. Take this big dick."

And, that I did. As he moaned sliding in and out of my juices, I was in my own world. "Fuck me! Fuck me! It feels so damn good," I moaned with him.

"You love this dick. Don't you?" He pounded harder and harder until I answered.

"Yes, I love this dick," I admitted, taking every bit of it.

"Whose pussy is this? Whose is it?" He was so cocky it turned me on more. If I wasn't doing a good job, he was surely a good actor.

"It's yours, Daddy. It's all yours."

"Turn around so I can get this ass from the back," he said flipping me all in one motion. He fucked me so hard from behind I had to throw it back. "Yeah, that's how you do it. Throw that ass back!"

"Oh, Oh, Oh, Oh," is all you heard from me.

It was hurting so bad, but at the same time, it felt so good. So this is what good sex felt like. I thought I felt it before, but boy, oh boy, was I wrong.

"Let me ride this dick, Daddy. It's my turn to work." I got on top and started doing my thing. That nigga was squirming like a bitch. Yeah, I said it cause I deserve my props.

"Damn girl, this shit feel so good!" he moaned. "That's right! Tame this dick. Put a claim on it." I watched his toes curl and the crazy expressions on his face. "Damn girl, where you been at? I aint never been fucked like this before."

"You got me now. I'm yours Key. I'm all yours." I felt myself about to climax again.

"I'm yours too, baby." He guided my hips up and down making sure every inch of him was inside of me. I knew my insides were punctured for sure.

I couldn't hold back any longer. "I'm 'bout to cum again." My whole body quivered uncontrolably.

I knew this nigga was special. *I don't even care if I don't see him again. At least I got to feel what good dick feels like. I'm lying. I'll kill him if he tries to play me.*

"Cum all over this dick, Skyy. Come on," he grunted.

I continued to move in motion.

"That's it baby. Keep it like that," he moved my hips faster and faster. "All shit girl, damn! I'm 'bout to cum," His voice cracked like he had a lump in his throat. I felt him growing inside of me as my head hit his sweaty chest.

I comfortably embraced his abs of steel as I remarked, "Now that was some good sex."

He was still trying to catch his breath. "Damn Skyy, you too young to be fucking like that."

"I told you I was a big girl. Didn't I?"

He cuddled behind me the rest of the night holding me in his arms. My thoughts were no longer could I handle the dick because I proved I could. But what the hell was I thinking not telling him to put a condom on?

*****

48

We got up, showered, dressed and checked out by noon. While crossing the Walt Whitman, I told Key to take me straight home instead of pass my Aunt Tee's house where my car was parked. As soon as we turned into the block, I noticed a lot of people and police cars surrounding the area where my house was located. Before thinking twice, I leaped out of the moving vehicle.

"Skyy, hold up a minute let me stop." Key yelled.

I continued almost falling to my knees. I spotted my parents speaking with two detectives and ran towards them.

My aunt, Shena, grabbed me in her arms. "Wait Skyy, calm down," she said.

I wiggled loose. "No, what's going on? Let me go!" I struggled with her. "MOM," I screamed, "Let me go. What's going on?"

My mom ran up to me full of tears. I grabbed her and broke down crying cause I felt something terrible was wrong. "Mom, tell me what's going on. Tell me what everybody is doing here."

"Come in the house."

"NO! Tell me what's going on." I cried out.

"Skyy, come in the house and calm down."

"Why won't nobody tell me what's going on? TELL ME!"

"Baby, something happened to Samir last night."

I broke past my mom screaming, "Where is he?"

My dad grabbed me into his arms and hugged me. "Skyy, hold up."

I lost all the feeling in my body and my knees hit the ground. My father then pulled me up into the house. "Dad, tell me where he is."

"Skyy," he paused. "They found him last night down the street outside his car." His eyes started to tear, but he wouldn't let a drop fall. That's just how he was. Always said he's too tough to cry, and he has to stay strong for the family.

I was confused. "Found him? What you mean found him?" My heart was beating out my chest.

"Somebody beat Samir really bad."

"He will be okay, right? Right, Dad? Please tell me he's gon be okay."

"He didn't make it. He died at the hospital." He grabbed me closer knowing I was about to lose control.

"No, please don't do this to me." I cried in his arms. "I should have been here. I should have been here." I repeated.

"Baby, you didn't know." He wiped my tears. "Stop crying. It's not your fault."

"Why him, Daddy?" I needed an answer. I couldn't understand why someone would do this to him. I don't even think he pissed a female off bad enough for his life to become a threat.

"We will find out. And whoever is responsible will pay."

"What am I suppose to do without him? He was my world. I can't live without him." I let go of my father and ran to my room.

"Lord, please tell me why. Why Lord?" I cried and cried. "He didn't deserve it. He didn't deserve to die. This can't be happening to me. Why me? Why Samir?" I cried until I soon drifted to sleep.

My mom woke me about eight that night. I was bawled up in fetal position not wanting to be bothered. The bedroom floor was a disaster from me knocking things over in a disrupted manner earlier when I found out the news.

"Get up and come eat something," she said, picking up perfume bottles to keep from stepping on them.

"I'm not hungry, Mom." I pulled the sheets back over my head.

She pulled them off me completely. "Skyy, please don't do this."

"I said I'm not hungry. Please just leave me alone right now." I began to cry again.

"I'm hurting too." She took a seat on the bed. "It's not your fault. Don't beat yourself up over something you had no control over."

"I told him to go out and get some air." I wiped my face. "This probably never would have happened."

"It's not your fault. Stop crying." She helped wipe my tears away.

"What are we gonna to do without him?"

"I don't know baby," she said, as she rocked and rubbed my hair. "Please come and eat something before you get sick. Don't shut yourself out from the rest of us."

"I'll be down. Let me get myself together."

"Alright, baby. I love you." She kissed my forehead and exited the room.

When she disappeared, I knew I had missed calls so I went to check them. There were seventeen new messages that I didn't feel like hearing, so I breezed through briefly. Several were from Key hoping I'd pick up. I didn't feel like talking, so I scanned through the rest and erased them all except for the last one, which was from Slim.

"What the fuck? He just don't get it do he?" I raged aloud. "Why won't he leave me alone?" After hearing the message, I saved it cause I had the same vibe from the last message. "What is the matter with that fool? He got serious issues. I wish he just get a life and stay out of mine." I tossed more things around the room angrily. My mom yelled for me from downstairs to hurry up.

Once I got downstairs, some of my family was still there sitting around gossiping. I sat over in the corner with my aunt Shena to keep out of sight. She was more like my sister than my aunt. We could talk about any and everything.

She came over next to me. "What's up, baldhead?" That was my nickname she gave me when I was little. "You feeling better?"

I wanted to say, *what do you think?* But bit my tongue. "You know how I felt about him."

"We're gonna get through this together, okay?"

I cradled my head with my hands. "I hear you, but I don't know about that. I can't even focus right now."

"You just need some time, you'll be alright. Here come your girls."

Kizzy and Armani came over and hugged me. "Ya'll been here all day?" I asked.

"Yeah, we were waiting for you to get up," Kizzy responded.

"Where is Mashae?"

"She went to get her daughter. She said she'd be right back." They both took seats beside me on the floor. "Jae and NeNe came by earlier to see you, but they left."

I was tired of associating already. I sat quietly feeling sorry for myself. My brother was gone and I didn't have anything else on my brain except being without him.

"Key was here for a good while too. He said call him when you get up," Kizzy smiled, thinking that was going to cheer me up.

If I weren't with him last night, maybe I would have been in the house with my brother. Thinking about it made me break down and weep. She started rubbing my shoulders.

"I don't feel like all that talking shit right now." I snapped at her feeling bad after I did, but she didn't get offended.

"I feel you. Just know we're here for you."

"Let me go get something to eat." I got up and headed to the kitchen eyeing Armani. "I hope your greedy ass aint eat up the kitchen." We all laughed.

We sat eating and talking about other things residing in our lives. Armani admitted accepting J.J back into her life. Mashae clued us in on this mystery man she'd been seeing for almost a month now. Kizzy distressed how Tyrik was still hanging out late, and when she answers his phone at night, the person on the other end hangs up. I was the next runner up to give an update.

"How was it last night, Skyy?" asked Armani, anxious awaiting my answer.

"I don't feel like talking 'bout it right now."

"Well, if it was good, talk about it. Might make you feel a little better."

"I can't even enjoy that good feeling I felt last night. Every time I think about it, I wish I was here."

"Stop doing that to yourself. It's not your fault."

"Stop saying that! I'm tired of hearing it." I went to put my plate in the trash. "Come on, I need some air before I have a serious break down."

We took a ride past Mashae's house to see what was taking her so long. *Honk...Honk...*"Maaassshha" Armani yelled out at the window.

Mashae came to the door. "Why the hell are you screaming outside my house like that?"

"Just come on with your slow ass."

"Wait!" She went back in to get her daughter. Five minutes later they both came out and got into the car. "Take me to drop my baby to her daddy."

As we circled the corner to her daughter's father house, I noticed Slim and a couple of his homies posted outside the Chinese store laughing and joking. "Aint that Slim?"

"Yeah, that's that crazy ass nigga," I mumbled.

"Does he still call you?"

"He calls and leaves messages, but I aint fucking with him no more."

"You better not decide to go get your ass kicked again," Armani advised.

"Okay, I get the point. Just keep going. Mashae, hurry up cause I don't want the fool to notice my car and come around here." She climbed out swiftly.

"I'm trying to hear about last night cause Key looked like he was on cloud nine when he was talking to me." They both sat upright ready for the details. "I know it's itching you to tell us?"

"I don't even know where to begin."

"How about the beginning, trick."

Mashae heard the topic as she got back into the car and said, "Just tell me if the rumor I heard was true."

I told the story beginning to end. After I was finished, everyone was speechless. "Damn, say something. Ya'll beat it out of me."

"That's some romantic ass shit," Kizzy said and we all burst into laughter. "So what you think? Is this the *One* this time?"

"You tryna to be smart, Kizzy?"

"I'm just saying…"

Armani cut in to reiterate for her. "What she's saying is this the same feeling you felt in the past?"

"Not at all. I feel different." These feelings were for sure nothing I have ever felt before.

"How different, Skyy? Didn't I tell you to control yourself?"

"And didn't I say I'm not as tough as you, Ms. Fuck 'em and leave 'em alone?"

"Hey, that's my *Mo'do*. And that's why I be having these niggas hurting instead of me." She reminded me of how I use to be. "They do it so why can't we? It's about to be a new millennium, and I'm about to change the game." If there was anyone to turn the tables, Armani was the one for the job.

"Your brother gon kick ya ass," Kizzy said looking like she just seen a ghost. "Aint this some shit?" We all looked out the windows to figure out what she was talking about. "This muthafucker is losing it."

It was Tyrik's car outside the same chick house that Kizzy almost killed the other day on 52nd Street.

"Chill Kizzy," I said making sure she didn't take a leap out the car again.

"You know what? I aint even gon trip. Take me home."

"You aint going home. Fuck him," Mashae spat.

"Take me home. Hurry up before he leaves." We did as told. She collected everything of his in the house from the pictures down to his dirty socks in the hamper.

"What the hell you 'bout to do, Kizzy?" The look on her face frightened me.

We followed her out the door. "Take me back around there." She placed everything in the trunk and got in the car.

"What are you doing with the club?"

"You think after the last time he would have got his act together, but he didn't. I guess I have to help him." She threw her hair back in her famous ponytail and tied her shoelaces tight.

Tyrik's car was still parked in the same spot. It was directly in front of the house where she lived. The lights were on down stairs but off upstairs, and both air conditioners, up and down, were on full blast.

Kizzy got out the car with the club and her knife. She successfully flattened all four tires. Next, she went around the whole car scraping it with the knife, and then this was the ultimate. She broke every window and mirror out, including the rear view and side mirrors. I popped the trunk and helped get all his things out. She threw them through the open windows, but wasn't done. I don't know where the banana and sugar came from, but it went down the gas tank and up the tail pipe. That car was totaled. What used to be a 2000 Mercedes Benz S 500 looked more like an average car from the junkyard.

Nosy neighbors came to the door being distracted by the racquet, but not one person called the cops. Tyrik must have been caught up in whatever her was doing because he wasn't one of the spectators.

"Skyy, give me your phone," Kizzy demanded, walking over to me. She went to knock on the door since his voicemail kept picking up. When he realized it was her at the door, he finally answered the phone.

"Baby look..." He tried to explain without her getting a word out.

"Look my ass, Tyrik. I aint even trippin' but your ass better come outside right now if you wanna see your kids again."

"You gon flip out soon as I hit that door."

"I promise you I won't." She was trying to reassure him, but he wasn't buying it after the last episode. "I just need you to come outside. And tell that bitch she aint got to worry about me no more cause it aint even worth me going to jail over her or you. I got kids to raise."

It took him twenty minutes to get enough heart to come outside, and when he did his whole face dropped after seeing what use to be his pimp mobile. I thought Kizzy was going to take his head off, but to my surprise, she really didn't act a fool. I guess she couldn't handle anymore.

Kizzy walked up to him with a smile and kissed him on the forehead. "Now baby, was the pussy worth all this?" She patted him on the head like a good little puppy dog and walked away.

We all were in tears from laughing at his stupid ass looking pitiful as ever. Instead of heading back to the house, we went down South Street to get some ice cream and joke about the whole thing. I was glad to see Kizzy smiling, and Lord knows I needed that laugh.

I dropped Armani off at J.J's house, Mashae back home, and saved Kizzy for last. We sat in front of her door a while talking. "Are you going to be alright by yourself, Kizz?" I knew she would break down once inside.

"I just don't understand it. What was I doing so wrong that he can just continue to say fuck me like this?"

"Stop blaming yourself. He's an asshole."

I myself couldn't understand why he did the things he did having the good girl he had. She gave up a lot for him. Even got him to where he is right now. Giving all her hard earned money and tax refund checks to pull weight. But what is there to understand? Men are going to be men and that's that!

"The bad part about it is you're absolutely right. He is truly a dickhead."

"So why do you keep allowing yourself to go back?"

"I can't answer that cause I don't know. It's like I know he's not shit, but I can't let him go."

"Is it because he's the father of your children?"

"No, it's because I love him too much."

I knew she wasn't lying. Kizzy never took this much shit from a nigga before. Little did she know she was way past the love stage.

"Love doesn't hurt, Kizz. Don't you think you deserve to feel that love back?" I looked her in the eyes trying my best to get through to her like she did for me. "It's been long enough for you to open your eyes and realize you deserve much more than you're getting."

"How were you so strong when you left Slim?"

"It's not all about being strong. It's about finding yourself, and I couldn't find it with Slim." I felt her pain and

I knew she wanted out, but you can't make a person leave until they're ready. "Remember, you were the one that talked me out of a horrible situation. Why can't you take your own advice?"

"I'm weak for this boy. It sickens me."

"It's time to think about what's most important in this situation and that's your kids."

"They deserve a father."

"You're right and they will have one, but that doesn't mean you have to keep playing the fool to keep him around." I was getting emotional so I paused to catch my breath "Tyrik loves his kids and will be there for them regardless of ya'll being together or not. Just let him move on and do his thing. Who knows, he might be ready to stop playing games and realize what he has and marry your crazy ass." We both laughed.

"You know I'm gonna miss Samir so much, Skyy." We all were pretty close being as though we were first cousins.

"I'm gon miss my baby too. I can't believe he's gone."

We wiped one another's watery eyes and hugged. "Stay here tonight, we both can use the company," she suggested getting out the car. I couldn't argue with that so I locked up and followed her in.

●● *Armani* ●●

I was back at J.J's house catching up on lost time. He was the one guy I could honestly say I fell head over heals for. After we split up, that's when I started doing things my way or no way at all. This is the type of affect a man can have on a woman.

59

"So what's up J.J?" I was wondering what he was back in town for.

He answered my question with, "Where you been, Armani? I've been looking for you for a few days now."

"I've been through a lot these last couple weeks, so I been staying to myself."

"So who's new in the picture?"

I know he don't call his self trying to ease back in my life after he rolled out on me to a whole new state with no forewarning. I wanted to say this out loud, but decided to hold it back for now and get some more questions answered. "Look, I aint come here to talk about another nigga. I came to see you."

"Well come here and show me how much you missed me."

I walked over to him steadily desperate for his tongue. He didn't waste any time undressing me. "Damn J.J, don't be ripping my shit off like that. Hold up!"

"C'mere, I miss you," he ordered, letting my shirt hit the floor. He was very familiar with all the weak spots, so he went straight for the most fragile.

He was eating my sweetness so good I yearned for more. "You eatin' my pussy so good," I whispered. "Oh my goodness..." Right in the middle of it all, there was a bang on the door. I pushed his face away. "Who is that banging like that?"

"How the fuck do I know? I'm up here with you." He got up and crept to the window.

"It's probably one of your raggedy ass bitches. I aint for this shit tonight. Damn, I should have kept my ass home." I placed my clothes back on and peeked out the window. "Who the hell are all those bitches?"

"She must have known I had company. She be stalking me and shit."

"She?" I gazed back at him. "I told you about messing with these gutter ass bitches." I mugged him and went to get my phone. "Get your mind right."

"I'm not trying to hear that right now, Armani. Be quiet and she might go away."

As soon as he said that, the chick banged harder screaming out, "Jayshon, I know you're in there with a bitch. I aint going no fuckin' where! So come on out. And call the police cause I don't give a fuck."

I gave a troubled look after viewing the time. It was just past three in the morning. Mashae's phone rang twice before she answered, then we called Skyy on the three-way.

"Skyy, get up. We have a situation." Bits and pieces were revealed before hanging up to be on their way. They decided the meeting place would be the corner of J.J's block.

Mashae brought her two cousins along for the help. Both cars were parked on the corner so them crazy bitches wouldn't try anything stupid and poke out tires or something.

By the time I got the call that they were at least on the block, my adrenaline was already skyrocket. I had already hit the top step before they had made it all the way down to the house. I gripped the female up that was making all the noise and punched her in the nose. She staggered back on the rail.

"Bitch, who the fuck is you?" another girl yelled out.

They didn't notice the rest of the crew coming up from behind. I ignored the question and hit the chick again. They all tried to jump on me. Kizzy ran up to first grabbing hold of one. She was destroying her, while Skyy and Mashae had shared another. Mashae's two cousins stood in the background holding the last girl by her throat. They told her she better not move and she obeyed.

After ten long minutes of fists, ass and tities flying in the air, we heard police sirens. We knew it wouldn't be long because he lived down in a quiet neighborhood. Before J.J went in the house and shut the door, he watched the hood rats jump in their car and pull off. Then advised we do the same.

"Damn, is this night ever gonna end?" Mashae examined a scratch on her face in the sun visor mirror.

"I don't think so cause it's too crazy."

"No, this shit is too hilarious," Kizzy said laughing.

"Kizzy, you always find shit like this amusing with your silly ass."

We all went back to Kizzy's house and crashed on the floor. I couldn't help but wonder what the rest of the summer would be like, so I sparked up general conversation to see how everyone else felt.

"What's the rest of the summer gon be like?" A pillow came flying at me in the dark to shut me up. "I'm serious. So much has happened in just a couple weeks, but we still have a couple months to go."

"I don't even care at this point. I don't even know what I want anymore, or where I'm headed..." Skyy replied.

That answer threw me off. "Don't start talking crazy, Skyy."

"I'm being real, I don't know."

"You're getting out of here come September. What will be the point of staying back and being miserable?"

"Who's to say I won't be miserable wherever I'm at?"

Mashae spoke her peace. "Skyy, please don't do this. We planned to leave together and be together after high school,

so that's what we're doing." That's been the plan for them since middle school. Even though Mashae decided to keep her baby, that wasn't going to stop her one bit.

"Mashae, just drop it. I'm going to sleep."

I rolled over to look the other way as the whole room went silent. Everybody fell asleep soon after. There was no way I was going to let Skyy do anything other than what she been waiting to do all the years I've known her. School was always her first priority and I loved that about her. And with me being the big cousin she always looked up to, I would have it no other way.

•• *Key* ••

I was sitting back doing what most men do. That was wondering what my next move should be. Skyy really did the damn thing to me in that hotel room. Even if I thought about leaving her alone, how could I do so at a time like this? She probably already blames me for keeping her out that night her brother died. It doesn't matter cause my lil Shorty aint got nothing to worry about. She's definitely gon be 'round for some time.

As soon as I plugged my phone into the charger it rang reading a private number. "Who this?" I answered.

"It's Latasha pussy," she said, in a nasty tone.

"Look girl, it's too early for the dumb shit." I was definitely irritated by the sound of her voice.

"Let me find out you went to AC and with who. I'm telling you…"

"You aint telling me shit." I cut her off. "I'm not for this right now. Bye!" I hung up knowing she'd call right back "What?"

"Oh, you hanging up on me now? So who is the bitch, Key?" she dug.

"I was sleep. I'll holla at you tomorrow or something."

This time when the phone rang back, I answered without looking at the ID. "Look Trick…"

It was Rome calling in, not Tasha. "Hold up brotha. I may be a lot of things, but a trick aint one of them," he laughed, knowing someone done pissed me off.

I was relieved after hearing Rome's voice. "I thought you was that crazy bitch calling back."

"Well, I called to find out about the other one."

"Who, Skyy?"

"Yeah nigga, give me the low down." He was anxious to know if I got in the panties or not.

"I was asleep. I holla at you…"

"Let me find out I done touched a soft spot."

I laughed it off. "I'm just tired."

"Whatever you say homie. You know I know ya."

"I'll hit you when I get up."

"A'ight nigga, hurry up cause I got some shit to tell you."

Rome ended the call leaving me curious to know what it could be this time.

Chapter 5

ENOUGH

E veryone was asleep until we heard Kizzy screaming from the top of her lungs. Should've known Tyrik would be back much sooner than later. I got up and stretched before heading out into the hallway to see what was going on.

"I said get the fuck out," echoed throughout the house. Kizzy stood between the hallway and front door pushing for him to leave.

I butted in. "Look Tyrik, she said go. Now go!"

"Mind ya business, Skyy." He gripped Kizzy by the arm trying to force her back inside.

"Let her go and get the hell out." I attempted to turn them loose from one another.

"Make me," he replied, giving me that scary look that scared everyone else. It didn't faze me one bit. I've been through too much to be scared of a nigga that bleed like I do.

"Look Tyrik, I aint trying to fight your dumb ass. That's all you know how to do is hit women. You's a bitch!" I spat.

"That's exactly why you use to get your ass kicked, cause you talk too much."

I knew Kizzy told him about all the incidents with Slim and I. She probably thought I was going to be mad at her after he said that, because she smacked him so hard it left a handprint.

That's the problem with people, like Tyrik in this case. You tell them something that's not suppose to go any further, but as soon as they get mad they use it against you as a weapon. He didn't appreciate that smack at all. He punched her in the eye so hard it landed her on the ground. That's when all hell broke loose. I don't know where Mashae and Armani came from, but Tyrik was on the bottom of the pile. He tried his best to get us off him, but couldn't do nothing with us.

"Ya'll crazy," he said, scrambling to get out the door.

"Get the fuck out, and if you come back you gonna see more than crazy."

Kizzy slammed the door and took flight into her bedroom. We all knew her and Tyrik would fight at times, but we were never there to witness it, which made her feel slightly embarrassed. I went into the bathroom to get a cold washcloth and joined her in the room.

"Kizzy, you alright?"

"I'm cool, Skyy. You know I'm use to this shit by now." She was looking in the mirror at her eye.

"That's just it Kizz, aren't you tired?" I passed her the cold cloth.

"I'm tired of being sick and tired," she admitted. She took a seat on the bed and placed the cloth over her eye to help the swelling.

"You'll be alright when that eye goes down." We both laughed.

"I'm sorry I told him your business."

"It's cool. I know you talk to ya man."

"But I shouldn't talk to him about things you come to me about. That should be between us."

"You right. I should kick ya ass," I joked and gave her a hug.

"I love you, Skyy."

"I love you too, Cousin." I pulled her off the bed. "Now get ya ass up cause I'm not for the depressed shit."

Armani called us from the living room to hear the latest word about Samir on Channel 10 News. The media blabbed on about him being a victim of a robbery, but the facts are still unknown. I knew that was bullshit. They always talking about stuff they don't have the answers to. There were still no suspects in custody.

I was frustrated by it all. "The police need to get off their ass and on their jobs."

"They always quick to harass innocent people while the guilty ones roam the streets."

I walked back into the bedroom to call my mom and see how she was holding up. "Hey Mom, what you doing?"

"Just getting these arrangements together."

"I'm at Kizzy's house if you need me."

"I already know. Armani called earlier and said you were okay."

I tried my best not to let her hear me sniffle.

"I love you baby. We're gonna get through this, okay? We have to sit down and have a heart to heart soon as we both get time."

The way she said that, I knew Armani had opened her mouth about what I said last night.

"Everyone is worried about you, Skyy. We just don't want to see you make any wrong moves."

"Alright, I'll talk to you later."

"Remember I love you," she said and I heard my dad yell, "I love you too baby," in the background.

Kizzy was calling out for me from outside to come to the door, so I cut the conversation quick to see who it could be. *I don't feel like this shit. Who is it now?* I wondered getting the shock of my life.

"Hey Shorty, how are you?" asked Key.

"Just had to find me, huh?" I grinned, shaking my head.

"You're acting like you don't know a nigga." He paused waiting for an explanation.

"I've been busy, Key." I instantly obtained an attitude. I didn't know why I was taking my frustrations out on him, but I was.

"Skyy, I know you're hurting. I just wanted to make sure you were cool."

"I'm said I'm okay. I'll call you when I get a chance."

"Damn, it's like that. What's wrong with you?"

"I just want to be alone," I lied. I needed for him to hold me so bad but couldn't form the words to say it.

"Just call me when you get time." He walked away astonished by my behavior.

I felt bad watching him get into his car, but I had other issues to be concerned about. I let him go and went back inside.

"Damn Skyy, you think you could be a little more sensitive?" said Mashae, with an attitude.

"What are you talking about?"

"He really cares about you. Give him a chance."

"Look, let me worry about it okay. I'm not for no relationships right now. I got other issues on my mind I'm more concerned about."

Armani started picking up the blankets from the floor and said, "That don't mean you have to act like a bitch about it."

I lost my cool. "Who you calling a bitch, Armani?"

I broke one of the main rules in our friendship. Never get offended!

"Calm down," Kizzy said, trying to take control of the situation.

"I'm tired of this shit. She always got something to say." I picked up my pocketbook. "Just worry about who you fuckin'."

Armani let the attitude fly by. "I'm not even gon there witchu cause I know your upset."

"Fuck being upset. I mean it, stay out my business!"

"I will stay the fuck out your business. Stop telling it to me," she snapped back with her hand in motion.

"Skyy, why you trippin'?" Kizzy asked, still trying to keep the peace.

"I'm tired of this shit and I'm tired of trying to figure out what the hell is going on around me."

Mashae decided to let her lips loose. "We're just trying to be here for you."

"I'm not talking to you, Mashae." I rolled my eyes and sucked my teeth.

"Well, I'm talking to you. You really trippin' right now."
"I'm keeping it funky."

"You keeping what funky?"

"I'm tired of this life and I'm tired of this dumb shit I got to go through day after day." I headed for the door. "Man, I'm out."

Kizzy tried to question where I was going, but I slammed the door in response. It was time to take a ride to cool off.

I found myself over at my Aunt Shena's house. I had a key so I went right in, finding her and her best friend Alicia at the dining room table sippin' on Bacardi Razz coolers.

"What's up baldhead?" They both embraced me.

"Ya'll always drinkin', let me get a swag."

"You better get away from my drink," Alicia warned me. "Where you coming from?"

"Kizzy's house. I had to get out of there before I exploded."

"What's going on?"

"I'm just tired of this stupid shi..." I caught myself. "Oops! My bad. I meant stuff we go through all the time. If it's not with one of our niggas, it's with a female the next nigga belong to." I took a deep breath and sat down. "I just don't know what to do anymore. I'm losing it and I don't know what I'm gon do without my brother."

"Skyy, we all know how close you and Samir were. Everyone will miss him, but you have to let go and live."
Shena sat down with me. "Don't lose yourself. It already took you forever to find." We both giggled. "You're about to go away to school and start a new life on your own."

"But I'm not even sure of that anymore."

"You're talking crazy now. What you mean you don't know?" asked Alicia. She was upset with the way I was talking. She too treated me as a niece, and I loved her just like an aunt.

"I can't focus right now." I threw myself back into the pillow soft leather sectional as tears began to trickle down my cheeks.

"Skyy, it's only been a couple of days. You're still hurting. Just give it some time and things will get better."

"I don't know where to go or what's the next move I should make."

"The first step is to make your way into the bathroom to get yourself together." Shena put my head on her shoulder. "Stop crying, everything is gonna be alright and stop snottin' up my T-shirt."

The three of us laughed and gave a group hug. I actually felt more relaxed after talking with them.

I went up to the bathroom to clean myself up. We sat and talked about everything new in my life from Key to the incident at Kizzy's house. Our relationship was so bonded, I even told them what happened on the AC trip with Key.

"I think I just need some time to myself to get my mind right," I confessed.

"You might be right. But you can't shut everybody out, especially not your girls. You know true friends are hard to come by."

"That's exactly why I don't have any," Alicia blurted.

"I'm gonna take the kids to the movies." I advised, tired of being cooped up in the house.

I got Shena's two boys together and left. Alicia followed me out to go pick up her own kids. The boys and I went to see *Toy Story* down on Delaware Avenue. They were as happy as can be.

After the movie ended, the boys and I were heading out the theatre when I noticed two familiar faces crossing my path. I could've hit the floor when I saw the person tagging along by NeNe's side.

"Skyy!" she smiled, and his chin hit the floor.

"Hey NeNe!" I looked over at him and said, "Hi Tykey."

NeNe had a confused look on her face, "Oh, ya'll know each other?"

I eyed Key heavily. "Yeah, we know each other real well."

She quickly changed the subject. "Aint these Shena's boys?"

"Yup," I said, still looking at him. I knew his heart was pounding by his silence. "Let me go so I can get them home before it gets too late." I grabbed both their hands.

"I'll stop by one day this week to check up on you," she advised, unaware of the pain revolving inside of me.

I didn't turn back as I walked away, but I could feel his eyes follow me all the way to the exit.

"Are you okay, Key?" she asked, waving her hand to get his attention.

"Yeah, yeah I'm cool," he stuttered.

"Is there something I should know about?"

"Nah Ma, everything is good," he lied and she knew it.

"So how you know Skyy?"

"We were friends." He knew she deserved more of an explanation than that weak one he'd just gave. "We went out a few times."

"And?" She gave a pregnant pause waiting for more details.

72

None came so she continued.

"How long ago was this?"

"Just before her brother died."

NeNe felt bad assuming I left the theatre thinking the worse, and she didn't get a chance to explain they were just friends.

"Damn, you know that's my girl, right?"

He answered in a low tone, "That was my girl too."

"Well, we're here now. Let's just go see the movie and call it a night. I'll go see Skyy tomorrow to clear things up."

Although Key had no idea NeNe and I were friends, he was on a real guilt trip at that moment. He wanted to go chase me down and say how he felt, but instead, he grabbed NeNe's hand and responded, "Come on, the movie already started."

The whole way to the car I was talking to myself cussing his black ass out. "I can't believe that pussy."

"Skyy, that a bad word to say," my little 5-year-old cousin said.

"I'm sorry baby, I didn't mean to say it." I started the car. "I don't believe this is happening to me. He's out with my girl while I'm sitting alone depressed." I took a couple deep breaths. "Get it together Skyy. Get it together." I proclaimed before pulling off.

I quit talking aloud but couldn't help but to think about it. *Why is this happening to me? How did they end up together? What if they had sex?* These are the questions I badgered myself with on the way home. It felt like my world was crashing down. *What's next? What else can possibly go wrong?*

When we returned to my aunt's house, it was hitting nine o'clock. I ran upstairs quickly to locate Shena.

"Auntie, guess who I saw at the movies?" I didn't give her a chance to respond. "Never mind, don't guess. Key was at the movies with NeNe."

"Little NeNe?" she asked raising her brows and continued to clean her bedroom.

"Yes!" I was looking for sympathy, but wasn't getting it there.

"Well, you don't want him," she bluntly replied.

I bawled my face up. "I never said that. I was just going through something and needed some time to myself."

"He's a man, and if you would have just told him how you felt instead of avoiding him, maybe he wouldn't be there with NeNe or anybody else."

I felt drained and bewildered. "I don't even care anymore. I'm tired of wrecking my brain all the time over nothing."

"That's your problem. You give up too easily."

"I'm not giving up. He was never mine to start with."

"How you know? After the first night ya'll spent together, you let him go without knowing what he wanted or how he felt." She stopped to collect some papers.

I was desperate for advice and upset her full focus wasn't on my issues. "What am I suppose to do?"

"For starters, go apologize to ya girls. Then you can work on getting ya man back."

"They know I was trippin'."

"They may know, but that doesn't mean you can't apologize for acting like a little bitch wit ya spoiled ass."

"There's that word again." We giggled in unison. I hugged my aunt feeling a lot better than I did when I first walked through her door.

I headed home instead of Kizzy's house. I just didn't feel like being bothered with it all right then. All night I cried and prayed asking the Lord to forgive me for all the wrong I've done and grant me the strength to get through this dark cloud. Hopefully, my prayers would get answered and he'll guide me in the right direction.

*****

It was now Thursday, July 8th, the day of Samir's funeral. It's only been about four days, but since he's Muslim he had to be buried quickly. The whole family was over waiting for the family limos to come pick us up. When I awoke, the first three people I saw lounging around my bed were Kizzy, Armani, and Mashae. My girls made sure to be by my side to help me through. We all hugged, cried, and told each other how sorry we were. They helped me get dress and we headed downstairs.

Everyone was gathered around hugging with very little tears. I thought my mom would have broke down by then, but she didn't. That was a sign, which made me feel deep down inside that everything would be okay. I saw Jae and NeNe sitting on the sofa waiting patiently for me to come over.

"Thank ya'll for coming." I greeted them both with warm hugs.

"You knew we would be here," Jae smiled. Samir gave her the nickname Smiley because every time he saw her, that's what she was doing.

NeNe pulled me to the side. "Skyy, I just…"

I put one finger up. "Shhh, it's okay NeNe. I know neither of you had a clue."

"You're right, but that's not what I wanted to say. If it makes you feel any better, Key and I never did anything."

I was happy as hell inside after hearing that. "I don't want to talk about this right now. We'll talk later."

"Okay, but let me just say this. After you left the movie theatre, a part of him left with you." I stared in silence as she strolled away.

"Come on everyone. The limos are here," my mom ordered, getting the family together.

Here we go, I thought to myself, took a deep breath and headed for the door.

The funeral parlor on 20th & Reed St. was swarming with unfamiliar faces. So many faces I'd never seen before. My brother had more love than I knew about. I stood between my mother and father as we proceeded in.

The funeral lasted about an hour and a half. I didn't really lose it until they started to remove the casket. That's when I broke down, which made my mom break down, then everybody else followed. My dad tried to hold us both up but couldn't handle it, so my uncles came to help.

Mashae came over and pulled me outside to get some air. "Take deep breaths, Skyy."

I heard another voice come over my shoulders and say, "Calm down, baby girl. It's gonna be alright."

When I looked up it was Key. He grabbed me close to him, which made me cry harder. The scent of his cologne made me realize what I'd been missing.

"Why me, Key? Why me?"

"It's okay baby. I got you now and everything is gon be a'ight. I'm gonna protect you, Skyy. I'll protect you forever no matter what."

That's the last thing I remember before passing out in his arms. I remember envisioning different people and things that had previously happened in my life. I also had a vision of my brother walking towards me with open arms. He advised he was okay and that it was time to pull myself together.

When I awoke, I was in my bedroom resting. My mom was putting the clothes away that she had washed for me the night before.

"Mom, how long have I been out?" I asked, recalling some of what happened.

"Only about two hours. Are you hungry?"

"I saw Samir, Mom. I'm not crazy. I saw him." My heart began to rush.

"I know baby. I saw him too."

"I'm serious. I saw him come to me."

"Baby I know, but it's time to pull together, especially at a time like this." She sat on the bed. "I want you to get focused and start thinking about you and what's good for you."

"I'm trying," I mumbled, lowering my head.

"Well, try harder because I'm not going to make you do anything. It's time you start making your own decisions so you can learn from your own mistakes."

"I was so excited to be heading off to college, but now it's like you need me here with you. I don't want to lose you."

"I'm not going anywhere. I'll be here whenever you come home. Skyy, it's time to live your life. I've lived mine, and trust me I'll be okay. Remember, I still have your dad here getting on my nerves." We shared a laugh.

"Mom, so much is happening so fast. I don't even know what's going on half the time."

"One thing I bet you do know is that fine looking young man downstairs that's been here waiting for you all day."

My eyes widened. "Key downstairs?"

"Yes, and if I knew you would've been this thrilled, I would've let him be the first person you saw when you got up."

"Oh no, we would have been fighting if you let him see me like this."

"Well get pretty and come down. Lord knows I'm tired of entertaining by myself. Everyone has been asking for you all day."

I pulled her shirt as she rose from the bed. "I love you, Mom."

"I know you do. Believe me. I know."

Ten minutes later, I got to the bottom step and there he was looking more scrumptious than ever. I was still mad at him, so I had to front a little.

"What's up Key? Where the girls at?"

He stood up. "They went out to ride on the bikes with Rome and them. I told them we would meet when you got up."

"I aint goin' nowhere wit you," I frowned.

"Don't start, Shorty." He sat me down.

"NeNe's my girl, Key. How you end up with her out of all people?"

"I didn't know. When I saw you, I could have died."

"I saw the expression on your face," I chuckled.

"It's a small world."

"That's right. So don't think you can do me greasy and get away with it."

"Did you forget that you left me hangin'?"

"No I did not. I just was going through a phase."

"Are you out of that phase?" he asked, squinting his eyes.

"Maybe," I smiled. "Maybe not."

"You know what girl? You got a lot of shit with you. Come take a ride with me."

"I have to eat something first. It feels like my stomach is touching my back."

"Go ahead, greedy. I know how you get down."

I laughed giving him a little gut shot. "You want a plate?"

"Nah, I ate already. I've been here for hours. Your mom took good care of me."

Just then I saw my Aunt Shena walking over. I knew she was about to start with the 101 questions. "I guess this is Key."

"Yes, I'm Key. Nice to meet you," he welcomed with a genuine handshake.

Shena was impressed. "Oh, he got manners. Yes, he's a winner."

I agreed without his knowledge. "Key, this is my Aunt Shena."

"Is this the crazy one you told me about?" he asked smiling.

"Boy, you done lost your brownie points already." We all laughed and my mom called me in the kitchen.

She informed me that Slim had just called her line, which is different from my bedroom number. I was shocked he had the balls, but appalled by the way she badgered me with questions.

"How did he get your number?"

"I was gonna ask you that." She placed her hands on her hips and gave a grimy look.

"I don't know. I don't even know how he got my number."

"I don't want him calling here."

"You think I do?" I asked, upset I was being interrogated.

"I told him you were busy so you couldn't talk. He said he would call back but I kindly asked him not to," she sighed, then paused, "If your father would have answered it would have been a mess. I wish you never had dealt with that boy. I knew he wasn't no good. Help me take these cakes out there."

After hearing that, I'd lost my appetite. "I'll be back later, I'm going to meet up with Kizzy and them."

"They rode off on motorcycles. You getting on one?"

"Yes," I stated. Although she hated the sight of me on one, she knew there was no keeping me away from them.

"Skyy, be careful!" she yelled out. "You know how I feel about those things."

"I will, Mom. I promise." I grabbed Key and flew out the door before another word could be said.

Rome was flying East on 76 Expressway with Armani on the back of his bike. "Damn Rome, slow down," she yelled, scared for her life.

"I thought you was a rider, Armani?"

"I am, but you ride like a fool."

"I know how to ride. Stop sweatin' me, boo." He was dodging in and out cars.

"Hold up! You left the rest of them," She said, trying anything to get him to slow down. All the time we been riding, I never knew Armani to be scared. He must have really been acting a fool. "Slow the hell down or let me off."

"A'ight, stop crying. I got to hit the gas station anyway."

A few minutes later the rest of the squad made it to the Hess gas station on Grays Ferry where they were filling up.

"Armani, I know you were snapping," Mashae smirked, pulling her helmet off.

"You know she was. I told her to cool out."

"Fuck that. Yeah, I was snapping cause you an asshole," she spat. Everyone burst into laughter. "The shit aint funny. Somebody switch rides with me cause he's a lunatic."

Rome disregarded the insult and reached for his ringing cell phone. He advised to Key where they were. We pulled in minutes later catching the end of Rome and Armani's dispute.

"What's all the fuss about?"

"This fool tried to kill me on the Expressway," she replied, slapping Rome in the back of the head.

"Rome, stop that shit a'ight," I snapped at him. I knew his crazy ass was doing some off the wall stuff. The stories Key told me about them two were outrageous. Rome's characteristic traits are on the level of a daredevil.

"I told her I would slow down. She shouldn't have said she was a rider."

"That doesn't mean act stupid," I said, giving a dirty look. He knew if anything happened to her on the back of that bike that would be the last bike he ever got to see again.

"Let's ride," Key said, putting my helmet back on.

As we pulled out of the Hess gas station, there that dark-blue Buick was again. "Shit! Shit!"

"What you say babe?" Key asked, turning around.

"Nothing, just go ahead," I told him trying to get out of there as quick as possible.

We took a nice long ride to Delaware and had diner at this Japanese restaurant where they cook the food in front of you. Before heading back, we also stopped for ice cream at Ben and Jerry's ice cream parlor. The ride after that was cool. I held on tight to Key enjoying the breeze. I had found my comfort zone. That was until...

Chapter 6

MOVING ALONG

I t was almost nine-thirty when we pulled up to Armani's house. "What you got to snack on in there Armani? I know ya greedy ass got something."

"Ya mama greedy," responded Armani.

"And ya momma always yappin'," he joked.

"That's exactly why I'm a buss you in ya head one day. Is everybody chillin' here or what? I got some drinks in there."

"Yeah, I guess so cause I got the munchies too," Key said on the same vibe as Rome.

We sat around crunching away and sippin' on Martinis Armani mixed up in the kitchen. "Let's play *Questions*."

"Armani, what the hell is *Questions*?" asked Key, never hearing of the game before.

"Skyy, give them the low down and I'll get the shot glasses."

I began to explain the rules. "The object of the game is to answer a question with another question. You can't laugh, hesitate or answer the question directly, or you'll have to take a shot."

"I know I'm 'bout to be tore up," he said. "That's not fair cause ya'll probably been playing forever, so ya'll pros by now."

"Maybe you getting drunk is a good thing so I can take advantage of you," I winked at him.

"Alrighty then, start the game. I like the sound of that." He sat slouched over not trying to give his undivided attention.

"Yeah, me too." Kenny agreed nodding at Kizzy. "Are you gon take advantage of me?"

"You know I am, boo. I'm about due for some dick," she bluntly admitted and we all burst out laughing.

I couldn't believe my ears. Kizzy hasn't been with another man since her second child by Tyrik, and that was three years ago.

In the middle of the game there was a knock at the door. When Armani came back in and looked at me, first person I thought of was Slim. I got up to see what he wanted before he tried to come in.

"What's up, Shorty?" asked Key, as I got up.

"Don't worry, let me handle it," I advised having Armani walk me outside.

"Wassup, Skyy?" Slim smiled soon as I hit the door. "Did ya mom tell you I called?"

"Yeah, she told me. You can't be calling her house like that."

"I just wanted to know if you were okay." He tried to sound concerned and sincere, but it wasn't working. I knew what he was there for, and it wasn't to make sure I was alright.

"You don't have to worry 'bout me, but thanks for asking. I have to go." I went to close the door, but he hopped up the steps and stopped me.

"Why? Who you in there with? These aint ya'll bikes."

"Slim, please not tonight. Just go," I begged.

"I'm not going anywhere until you tell me what's up."

"I told you already. It's over! Why can't you just leave me alone?"

"Cause I told you before you still mine. You in there fuckin' that nigga?"

When he asked that, it seemed more like a statement than a question. He gripped me up by my collar and swung me down the steps. Armani called out for the rest of the crew and they came running.

"Damn Slim, why you got to come around acting a fool all the time?" asked Mashae, busting through to get down the steps.

"Shut the fuck up Mashae and mind your business."

Key trailed two steps behind her. "Yo, let her go!" he demanded, while staring Slim down hard.

"Oh, so this is who you in there with. Mr. NBA himself."

"Let her go, Slim," Key repeated balling his fists. I dropped my head hoping it wasn't about to go that far.

"Nigga, don't be calling me by my name like we friends." Slim dragged me a few more feet towards his car. "You found your meal ticket, huh? Is that why you been dissin' me?" I tried and tried to pull away but the hold was enormous. "I asked you a question bitch." His smack was so firm it made the whole right side of my face numb.

Key leaped over me and hit Slim with a three piece. Slim's homie jumped out the car having 8 against 2. Yes, all of us tore them up together with little damage being done to Key and his squad, but Slim and his homie really got their asses kicked. I knew that wasn't the end of Slim. Oh no, I knew him way better than that. But what I didn't know was when and how he would come, when he came.

We all went back inside with nothing but silence and movement filling the air. Crazy ass Kenny came out of nowhere and said, "Fuck that! I'm still trying to get drunk so I can get taken advantage of." That was the breaking of the ice for us all gaining back the mood. I grabbed Key's hand and walked him in the back bedroom with me.

"Hey, where ya'll goin'? It aint crunch time yet," teased Rome.

"Armani, please tame ya man," I said, as I shut the door.

She slapped him on the butt. "Sit down and be a good boy."

"Roof! Roof! Mommy," he barked like a dog. They all continued on playing the game where we left off.

"Key, I pulled you back here to explain what just went on, even though I don't know why myself."

"Skyy, it's not much you have to say. I already know about Slim."

"How?" I questioned embarrassed of him knowing how Slim treated me dirty a number of times.

"I know Slim from the streets, and I always heard about this young girl he was all crazy about," he said, massaging his chin. "But, I never knew it was you. I also know why you left him. That's what he's known for." He referred to the abuse and started caressing my cheek. "I'm glad he fucked up cause I wouldn't have the chance to be here with you right now."

I looked away and started crying thinking about what I just got him into. I didn't have a clue what Slim was going to do to this boy, or even worse, to me.

"Stop crying, Skyy. I told you I got you. Do you remember what I said to you at the funeral before you blacked out?"

"Yeah, I remember. You said you would protect me."

"Do you believe me?"

I remained silent scared to answer. I was afraid to be wrong because how can someone protect me from a psycho like Slim.

"Do you believe me, Skyy?"

Even though I was unsure, I still answered, "Yes, I believe you."

He brought my body close to his and kissed me. He undressed me gradually from head to toe. As he placed himself inside of me I began to quiver with glee. The sexual feeling I had was even better than make up sex, and that is supposed to be the best.

"Damn Key, it feels so good."

"I know you like it, baby. Tell me how much you like it."

"I love it, Key. I love it and I love you." *Oh shit, did I just tell this nigga I love him?* I said to myself. *Yes I did. What is wrong with me?*

Never have I been in a situation where someone made me slip and say I love you, especially during sex, but never say never.

He kept stroking in and out so passionately, holding me in his arms, and knowing the right moves to make. "You mean it, Skyy?" he whispered, as he continued to drive me crazy.

I knew if his shot was like this, his daddy had to be a killer.

"Yes baby, I love you so much." I figured what the hell, I already done slipped up and let the cat out the bag. "Just keep giving me this good loving like you're doing."

"I will. It's all yours so take it, baby."

This time, we both climaxed together. I swear if this feeling wasn't love, it wasn't far from it. We cuddled in one another's arms talking the rest of the night and laughing at all the weird noises coming from every other room in the house. I told him about me leaving in September for Howard University to major in nursing, and he advised of his move to Miami, Florida to start practice for the season.

"Skyy, you know you told me you love me, right? Was that in the heat of the moment?"

"Maybe it was, but I can't say that it ever slipped out before."

Generally, I was used to sleeping until mid afternoon when we have little slumber parties, but Armani had other plans. The next morning, she came banging on the door for us to get up and eat.

"It's only nine o'clock." I wiped the drool from my mouth hoping Key didn't see it.

"I cooked all this breakfast. Ya'll better get up. There's some new toothbrushes in the cabinet cause I know all ya'll breath stinkin'."

I went into the kitchen after coming out of the bathroom to get a woof of the aroma. "Damn, that must have been some good dick you got last night. You cooked all this?" I observed the pancakes, French toast, eggs, bacon, grits, sausages, and home fries. Rome was packing his plate with no one else in mind. "Save some for ya homies."

"They better hurry up."

"Let me make my boy a plate now, greedy ass."

Everyone sat around eating. There wasn't a word being said. All you could hear was the sound of jaws moving. I decided to spark a conversation tired of the smacking going on.

"What's up for today?"

"I don't know. Let's do Dorney Park or something." Rome suggested.

Armani agreed. "That's a good idea, but ya'll better go get dress now cause I aint heading out all late."

"If we take the bikes, it won't take that long to get there." "Armani, this some good shit." Kenny chewed away not thinking about nothing but what was on his plate. "Kizzy, can you cook like this?"

All us girls started laughing. "Inside joke fellas," Kizzy frowned not wanting to tell them why.

Rome tapped Armani. "What's the joke? I want to hear."

I told them the story about when Kizzy tried to bake chicken for the first time and put so much water in the pan that all the chicken was floating when I took it out the oven, and everyone fell out.

"Was it done?"

"Hell no! It wasn't done."

"So what! Fuck ya'll!" Kizzy said, laughing with us.

Armani advised someone's phone was ringing in our room and I offered to go get it. "Nah, I got it." Key got up from the floor and trotted into the bedroom.

The caller ID was marked private. Usually he doesn't answer those calls, but decided to anyway. It was Latasha calling to harass him again.

"What's up, Tykey?" He was shocked to hear her voice. "So, her name is Skyy? Didn't I tell you I would find out, pussy?" she snickered in his ear. He hung up, but she wasn't done.

"Stop calling my phone," he spat, filled with rage.

"When I see the bitch, you won't be able to recognize her the next time you get to."

"Fuck with her and watch she fuck ya dumb ass up. Now stop calling me," he warned and hung up again this time turning the ringer off.

"Who you cussing out?" asked Kenny, catching the tale end.

"Tasha, that bitch won't stop calling me."

"You better say something before she try some slick shit. You don't want her running up on Skyy and she don't know who she is."

"Yeah, I know. I'm tired of messing with these stupid ass hoes, Kenny." He threw his phone on the bed. "It's time to get my act together before I roll out."

"You found you a good one. Better keep her, you know they're hard to come by."

"If only I'd found her sooner." They both ended the conversation and came back out to join the rest of us.

We decided to make our destination for the day Great Adventures. When the guys left, we helped Armani clean the kitchen and straighten up. My mind drifted on how serious things were getting with Key and I. Everything just seemed too good to be true. It's only been a short amount of time we've known each other, but I felt like he was so right for me. Only time would tell, and the truth would surface soon enough.

Chapter 7

CONFESSIONS

After cleaning, we hung around feeling a bit lazy after that big breakfast we'd just ate. I watched as Armani skimmed through her rack of clothes in her walk in closet.

"Skyy, what you wearing?" she asked, pulling down hanger after hanger.

"I don't know yet. We gon be on the bikes so I wanna be comfortable."

"Kizz, what you wearing?"

"That big ass grin she had on her face all morning," giggled Mashae, pinching her cheeks.

"Shut up," she responded, defending her blush.

"I guess somebody got it in good last night, so come on with the juice," I provoked, but she acted as if it was nothing.
"Stop frontin', Kizz. He tore that ass up didn't he?"

"Kenny almost killed my ass, but it was good," she admitted. Her blush expanded.

"I guess that makes two of us cause Key did the thing to me too."

"These niggas got ya'll noses wide open," Armani said, like we didn't hear her down the hall begging for mercy.

"Armani please. You're the one up at six in the morning preparing pancakes and French toast. When the hell you ever made cakes and toast at the same time?"

"Anyway..." she began, but I cut her off before the lies came.

"Anyway nothing! What's the deal whore?"

"Rome is cool, but you know I have to take it for what it is."

"Be careful cause that nigga act like he aint got all his marbles."

"He had some extra marbles last night, goddamn."

"Let's go get dressed before they get back. Armani we be back. Please be ready."

I dropped Kizzy and Mashae off home and went to get dressed. We all lived a pretty fair distance apart, so it didn't take much time. When I got in the house, my mom and dad were on the sofa having a deep conversation. I kissed them both.

My mom had a worried look on her face. "Skyy, sit down for a minute."

"Aw Mom, please not right now. We're on our way to the amusement park," I pouted.

"One minute, Skyy."

"Oh boy, that means an hour," I mumbled, under my breath.

"Skyy!" she insisted, so I knew it was serious.

"Alright, alright. What's wrong?"

"Someone that was here last night told us they saw you talking to Slim outside the house a few nights back."

"He was out front when I came home to grab something."

"What did he want? Are you still dealing with that boy?"

"Mom, he was out there. What was I suppose to do." I looked at my dad to cut in and help me out a little, but he was looking pretty vexed himself.

"I was told it didn't look like you wanted to be bothered," he intervened.

"Daddy, it's okay. I can handle it." I feared for my father to get involved because Slim doesn't play fair, but my dad is on a whole different level. He doesn't play at all.

"No! How about I'll handle it."

"It's a done deal," I lied. "I told him it's over."

"You told him that before and he's stalking you now," my mom cut back in. "If something was going on, would you tell us?"

I had the chance right then to tell everything. About the messages, the fight last night, and how Slim keeps harassing me, but I didn't tell them anything.

I looked my mom right in the eyes and answered, "Yes Mom, I would tell you if something was wrong. Now I'm going to get dressed before ya'll make me late for my date." I kissed them both on the forehead and headed for the stairwell.

My dad grabbed me by the arm. "You know how much I love you, right?"

"Yes Daddy, I know."

"Well don't lie to me. I'm here to protect you." He kissed me and let me go on.

I blasted my Biggie (Ready to Die) CD as I got dressed. I started getting emotional because Samir and I would go back and forth with the verses to see who messed up first, which he always won. I looked up and said, "I miss you, baby boy. Please help me get through this. I need you." I felt his presence all over the room until the phone rang snapping me out of it. It was Mashae rushing me as usual and letting me know to pick them up from Kizzy's house.

When we arrived back at Armani's, the bikes were already parked outside. What was supposed to take us an hour to do wound up taking two, so I knew the guys were inside getting impatient.

"Damn, females aint never on time." Rome commented, as we walked in the door. "Are ya'll ready now?"

"Yeah, let's go. Don't make me fuck you up today," Armani warned him, but he didn't respond. "You hear me? I'm not kidding."

"I got you baby. Just be easy."

We all got on the bikes and headed for the Walt Whitman Bridge ready for the quick adventure.

By the time we got back from Great Adventures, it was almost eleven. We all pulled up to Armani's house tired and ready to hit the sack.

"Damn, I'm tired as hell," Key said, pushing his bike on the pavement. "Skyy, you rolling out with me?"

"Why? What's up?" I asked yawning.

"I just need to holla at you about something."

"Give me a minute." I went inside to see what the rest of them were doing for the night, but they all decided to lay back and chill.

We headed straight to Key's house from there. I held on tight with my head pressed against his back enjoying the ride. When we got a few houses down from his, I could tell something was wrong by the way he tried to make a sharp U-turn. I elevated my head after hearing a female screaming from down the block running for her car.

Key ignored her and kept riding. The U-turn had slowed us down a bit, and I wanted to know what the hell was going on. I raised the lens to my helmet advising he stop the bike immediately. "Nah, that chick is crazy."

"Key, stop the bike or I'll get crazy."

He pulled over at the next corner allowing her to catch up. She pulled across from us and parked. "Won't you go ahead with that shit, Tasha!" He took his helmet off.

"Didn't I tell you I was gonna catch her?" She eyed me ridiculously.

"You caught me so now what?" I asked, offended by her threat.

She pulled out a can of mace that was in her hand and tried to spray me. I knew she had some slick shit up her sleeve, so I saw it coming and turned away just in time. Key smacked her and she hit the ground.

The unidentified female that accompanied her picked her up from the ground. "Why the fuck you hit her?"

"Mind ya business, Tiff. You aint got nothing to do wit it." Key continued to slander Tasha.

"Fuck…" Tasha started to get smart but my fist in her mouth stopped the comment.

It didn't stop there. After I got a few more jabs in, Key grabbed and lifted me off the ground. I got off one more kick to her chest before he restrained me completely.

"Hold up, Skyy. They don't want no work for real," he remarked, pushing me over towards a fence. "Tasha, roll out."

"Fuck you!" she yelled, then smiled at me. "Did you tell her we still fuckin'?"

"When bitch? Cause he been tied up wit me." I didn't buy into her act.

"So, that don't mean he aint have time to come fuck me," she smirked and swung at the same time. The blow caught me in my cheekbone. Both females then tried to jump on me. Key tossed them aside like he was Super Man.

"Oh, ya'll want to jump me?" I tried to get at them but was succumbed by Key.

"No Skyy, you don't need to be fighting."

" Let me go!" I tried to break loose.

When they came at me again, Key finally let me go, grabbed hold of the girl Tiff, and let me whip Tasha's ass. She got tired of me ramming her head into the side of a parked car and gave up.

"You wanna play like this, Key? You better watch ya back! Both of ya'll," said Tasha, trying to catch her breath.

They got in the car and sped off.

"Skyy, I'm so sorry," he apologized.

"An *Ex* right?" I smirked.

"Yeah, she's throwed off."

"I know the feeling." We got on the bike and rolled out meeting our destination at last to get some rest.

The insiders scoop was on from there. We laid on his pillow top king size bed as he told me all about Tasha. He admitted taking her personal until we bumped heads. I asked him what made me so special, but he couldn't answer the question, which made me wonder. All he could say was that he had a good felling about me. A feeling he didn't want to lose.

I put two and two together and assumed she was the one in the background the night we went to AC. The way I heard that smack through the phone, he must be feeling some type of way about me. That is unless he was just trying that hard not to ruin his chance at getting me naked.

I broke down and told him everything about Slim. I didn't feel humiliated when telling how Slim use to beat on me, or how many times I caught him in the bed with another chick. For some reason, I felt more comfortable in his presence. It was like I could confide in him and he wasn't going to do anything to hurt me. I've been wrong before, so I'd just have to see how right or wrong I was that time.

Chapter 8

PARTY TIME

hings were going smooth as the weeks floated on by. I haven't heard from or seen Slim, and there was no retaliation done after the fight as of yet. It was now July 23, 2000, my 19th birthday. I spent the night with Key to bring the day in with him. Early that morning my cell phone rang waking us both.

"Don't answer it. C'mhere!" Key pulled me closer to him in bed. "Happy birthday to you..." he sang, while playing touchy feely with me.

"What you want? A repeat from last night," I asked, nibbling on his ear.

"You know I do," he admitted. His phone rang next. He rolled over to answer. It was Armani on the other end. "Why you calling here so early? We were busy."

She paid him no mind. "Put Skyy on the phone for a minute."

"Here, it's Armani." He tossed me the phone and got up.

"What girl?"

"Do ya'll ever take a break?" she exhaled. "Happy birthday. We're trying to go to breakfast. We want ya'll to go."

I became frustrated because I was ready to get my groove on. "Why?"

"Come on, Skyy," she whined.

Rome snatched the phone to give his two cents. "Happy birthday Skyy. Where that lazy nigga at?" I abruptly passed Key the phone. "What's up, dawg? You tryna do breakfast?"

"I was just about to when you called," Key stated, informing him of his blocking.

"Look, Skyy's mom wants us to stall her all day so they can get the party together."

"I'm good at that."

"Handle ya business. Just call us when you done so we can go get something to eat."

Talking about eating was making me hungry, so I advised we get up and go. Key's response was, "Come here so I can fill you up."

We goofed around for another hour and a half before they began ringing our phones again. "It's Rome," he said after looking on the caller ID. He opened the flip and said, "Dawg, we getting dress now."

"We leaving ya'll. Meet us down at the South Street Diner."

Key agreed and tossed the phone aside to continue where we left off. A half hour later, we got up and dressed after working up major appetites.

"Where my present at?" I asked, anxious to find out what he got me.

He had already decided he was going to play with my emotions. "What present?"

"Stop playing. What you get me?" I poked my lips out like a baby.

"I just gave it to you. What, that wasn't enough?" I continued to whine. "I'm not kidding," he stated grabbing me into an oblique stance. "Alright, I'll give you some more of this good loving later."

I hit him and proceeded to put my clothes on. "What's up for tonight?"

"I don't know. What you wanna do? It's your day."

I want to know what the hell you got me, I thought but replied, "It doesn't really matter. I'm used to having boring birthdays."

"I guess we have to spike this one up cause I'm not a boring dude." He assured me this would be a memorable one as we kissed and headed out the door.

Armani and Rome were already eating when we got to the diner. I felt a lot of attention while walking pass tables to get to our own. One female even had the nerve to stop Key and ask for his autograph, which gave me an attitude cause she sneered at me. But what could I say? I was on his arm so she could make all the faces she wanted until her cheeks fell off.

I slid into the booth opposite Armani and Rome. "Ya'll couldn't wait for us?"

"Hell no! I told ya'll I was hungry." Rome responded.

"What's up for today, Skyy?" Armani wondered. "Let's go to Kopas and get some drinks."

"Or we could go to the mall and spend up ya'll money," I suggested.

"Good idea," agreed Armani. She looked down patting Rome's pockets.

"You know what? I'm a let you do that cause it's ya birthday." Key shocked the hell out of me. I was just joking, but I didn't let him know that.

"Well, it needs to be my birthday everyday."

"It's not, so don't get use to it."

We headed to the Cherry Hill Mall over New Jersey to do some shopping. Men hate shopping with females and I knew it, so I took advantage of this outing best I knew how.

"Skyy, don't get ridiculous," said Key, tailing behind me into all the stores.

By the time we finished, we both had them ready to kill us. "Where are ya'll going now?" asked Rome, looking worn out.

"Hold up Key, these shoes match my bag."

"You already got some to match every set you got. What the hell you need them to match a pocketbook for?"

"It's a girl thing." I kissed him on the cheek and disappeared inside the shoe store. "This is the last stop, okay?" He was outraged, but I aint care. It was my day. "Armani, these match perfect with the shirt you just got."

"Rome?" she called out from inside the store.

"Rome nothing," he mumbled, walking towards the exit.

"Okay, make sure you have that same attitude tonight," she advised, which captured his attention.

He made a 180-degree turn and passed her off some more money. I was in the corner snickering at his weakness. I searched my bag to locate my ringing phone.

"HAPPY BIRTHDAY," Kizzy and Mashae yelled at the same time. They had me on a three-way call. "Where you at?"

"The mall with Key, Armani and Rome."

"Spend that money. What we doing tonight?" Kizzy asked, as if she didn't know what was planned.

"I don't know yet. I'll keep ya'll posted."

"Tell Armani that J.J came by here for her."

I let that go in one ear and out the other. I knew how Armani felt about him, but I couldn't stand to see him do what he did to her again. I decided to keep that to myself. Besides, Rome had her time occupied well enough. We ended the call deciding on meeting up later.

Key was on my head as soon as I hung up. "Who was that?"

"Mashae and Kizzy. Let's go so I can lay down for a while." I looked over at Key. "I got a feeling it's gon be a long night."

"You right, Shorty. It's gon be a long one," he smiled.

Key woke me up at approximately nine-thirty that night. I was upset because I slept the whole day away, and after looking at the missed call list on my cell read zero, I felt like no one cared enough to say happy birthday.

"Why you let me sleep the day away like that? I didn't even go home to see my parents," I asked, jumping out the bed.

"I talked to them. They told me to let you sleep." He was drying off with a towel, and I wanted to jump all over him. "Get up and get dressed so we can go."

"Go where, Key? It's gonna take me an hour to get ready and all the restaurants will stop seating people by then."

"Who said we we're going to eat? Just hurry up and get dressed."

After hopping out the shower, I slipped on my white fitted halter dress that Key had just bought. It was more of a silky soft material with a diamond oval cut out in the front to show the little cleavage I did have, and another around my pierced bellybutton. The right side stopped just past my booty, and the left hung about five inches longer. Key was displeased when I tried it on at the store because of how sexy it was styled, but I talked him into getting it anyway. To top it off, I put on my white stiletto sandals with diamond cuts in the front and straps that tied up to meet my calves. My hair was pushed back out of my face with a fresh perm making it look as if I had Indian in my family.

"Damn, you look good girl," he exclaimed, spinning me in circles.

"And you didn't want me to get it," I smiled.

"We 'bout to take it back before somebody tries to steal you."

I hugged and kissed him giving off the props he deserved as well. "You know you're looking good yourself. What you so jiggy for?"

"How can I let you look all good by yourself?" he questioned, while answering his phone. "Yo, what's up?" he paused. "Yeah, I know. We're getting ready now." Another pause. "Got ya!" He ended the call.

I felt something sneaky was going on behind my back, but I didn't know what. I found out later the call was from my mom ordering him to get his ass there now or she was going to kick it.

"Who was that?"

"Rome! They're gonna meet up with us later."

"Aww man," I said, looking in the mirror. "I got to go home and get my jewelry."

"Don't trip babe. I got you." He pulled out these dangling diamond earrings that hung down two inches away from my shoulder. It had the matching diamond bracelet and necklace as well.

"Key, what, I mean who, how," I stuttered unable to find the words.

"Happy birthday, Skyy." My hug was filled with joy. "That's where Armani snuck off to down at the mall when she said she had to use the bathroom."

That sneaky winch, I thought to myself. He put the necklace on while I did the earrings. "It's so beautiful, Tykey."

"This is just the beginning of it," he assured me.

"I guess I have to show you later how much I thank you," I said, rubbing him down below. The lump began to swell.

We kissed and I even tried to seduce him, but of course my mom's demands were ringing through his ears. "I guess you do. Let's go! We got all night for this."

I tried contacting everyone on their phones as we drove to our destination, but no one answered. "Damn, where is everybody?" I threw the phone back into my purse.

"They probably can't hear the ring." He made excuse after excuse, which made me more suspicious. "Your mom and dad said they were heading out to dinner."

"They aint even call and wish me a happy birthday."

"Come on, Skyy. Stop acting like a bratt." He tried to shut me up, but I talked his ear off the whole ride.

Minutes later, we pulled into the Adams Mark Hotel on City Line Ave. It was a major crowd outside the front entrance. There were cars parked everywhere and a number of cliques standing around talking and smoking.

"Why you bring me here?"

"My homie is having a little engagement party. I told him I would stop by."

"I'm not trying to be here too long. I don't know these people."

He walked around to open my door and escort me out. "A'ight, just come on."

When we walked into one of the Ballrooms, all I heard was "SURPRISE!" I got choked up and almost hit the deck. "Happy Birthday to you…Happy Birthday to you," they sang to me as I scanned the room. Everybody was there. Even people I knew had beef with me came out to participate and find somebody to take home. Then I spotted my mom and dad as Key held my hand to guide me over.

They both hugged me. "Were you surprised?"

"Is that a trick question? You saw me almost faint." I was smiling so hard it was difficult to stop. I whispered in Key's ear, "I'll take care of you later."

He smiled and pulled me to the dance floor. On my way, I hugged and kissed all my relatives. "Hey Q! I'm glad you made it."

"You think I was gon miss this," he said, giving me a hug.

All my girls came up to tell me happy birthday. "I don't believe you whores kept this from me."

"We don't have to tell you everything. Some things are better left unsaid."

"I'm gonna remember that." I turned behind me to greet others. "Hey ya'll." I hugged both Jae and NeNe.

NeNe looked up at Key and said, "Hey Key."

"What's up NeNe?" he responded, in a low tone.

It felt a little uncomfortable, but I wasn't going to let that ruin my night. *He's mine now,* I thought swaying to Stevie

Wonder's (Happy Birthday) song. They all pushed me to the middle of the dance floor by myself. I'm glad I took a couple shots of Vodka before leaving Key's house, because I was ready to tear it up. I felt the eyes of all the haters burning holes through my clothes, which made me shake my tail feather harder. Key came out during the last bit of the song to dance with me. I really felt the fire then.

After the song died out, we had a moment of silence for my brother, Samir. Everyone put their lighters in the air. "I wish he was here," I mumbled.

"He is here, Shorty. He's in your heart."

I put my hand over my heart and looked up to the sky. "I love you, Samir."

Everyone was having a hell of a time. Free food and open bar all night, so you know the moochers were out. This had to be the best day of my life. I sat down with my parents and thanked them for everything. They told me it wasn't all their idea. I had to thank Key because he was responsible for most of it, including the bill. I looked over at him on the dance floor acting silly and thanked God for the wonderful blessing he had given me. The remainder of the night was beautiful being as though everyone acted like they had sense for once. Was that the best day of my life? No, it was the beginning of a new one!

*****

It's been almost a week since my birthday party. For some odd reason I'd been spending a lot of time up under my mom than usual. It felt like her presence was needed. I figured it was because I was leaving soon. Although I wasn't traveling too far away, I never been without my parents for more than a week before.

My mom came in my bedroom yelling for me to get up, but I wouldn't budge. "Skyy, get up," she continuously demanded.

I turned over the other way.

"Girl, get your butt up. You've been sleep all day."

I still didn't budge.

"Skyy, get up. Key is on my phone." She pulled the sheets back from my face.

"Why didn't he call my line?"

"He said you didn't answer. Now get up. Why are you always sleeping anyway? I better not find out your ass is pregnant."

"Aint nobody pregnant, Mom. Dang! Can you tell him to call my phone please?"

"Here are the pictures from the party. I'll set them on the dresser."

I jumped up excited to see the pictures. "It took you a whole week to get them out the film shop."

She ignored my comment knowing I was just as big a procrastinator as she was. "I cooked, so come get something to eat," she advised, before walking out the room.

I flipped through the pictures smiling at the ones with Key and I. Minutes later he was ringing my phone. "Why you still sleep?" he asked sounding lonely.

"I'm just tired. What's up?"

"Just wanted to let you know I'm flying out to Miami tomorrow."

"For what?" I asked, hoping it wasn't for more than a day.

"I have to go sign in and handle some things before the season begins."

"Oh, I'll see you when you get back."

"No you won't. I got you a plane ticket too. I want you to meet the team."

I wanted to scream, but I waited until we hung up to do that. "What time I need to be ready?"

"Just come and stay with me tonight cause I'm not sure yet. The time slot is open."

"I'll be over there after I eat. Do you want a plate?"

"You're gonna be my plate." I blushed without his knowledge. "Yeah, bring me one. You got the key to get in."

"Yeah, I got the key," I repeated.

"Aint that something. What you doing to me girl?" He snickered surprised himself.

"Nothing you don't want me to do." I hung up the phone and screamed downstairs for my mom.

She came running upstairs. "What Skyy? Why you screaming like that?"

"Key brought me a tick..." I began to explain, but she advised he'd already asked her permission. "What he ask you for?"

"Because he has manners."

"No, he's trying to score points. Daddy knows?" I was wondering if he was okay with it.

"Yes, he knows. He likes Tykey, but you know he still threatened him."

"Oh my Gosh. What am I gonna wear? You should've told me so I could've got my hair done, my nails..." I went on and on.

"Skyy, calm down. Everything is fine. Did you forget you just got everything done last week for your birthday?"

"Mom, that was a week ago. Everything needs to be fresh for a trip like this."

"Girl, take a chill pill."

"Mom please, don't nobody even say that anymore."

"What? It sounds corny?"

"Yes, and you sound real corny saying it." We shared a laugh.

I called Armani, Kizzy, and Mashae to come over and help me pack. They were there in like 6.2 seconds, not literally, but they got there pretty quick.

"Girl, pull out everything from jewelry down to sandals," they advised.

My room looked like a tornado hit it by the time we picked out everything.

"Bring me home a couple of numbers," said Mashae.

"Mashae, you aint never gon change."

"Well, neither am I. Bring me home some too," said Kizzy thinking the same. She shook her head in disbelief while pulling my suitcase from the shelf. "Who would have ever thought you would have this nigga hooked like this?"

"It looks like to me they got each other hooked." I frowned at the statement. "Skyy, sit here in my face and tell me you don't love this boy."

"I'm not 'bout to sit up here and say I do. It's only been a month and a half."

"And? Love don't have no date and time on it."

"I know, but how I fall so fast?"

"It don't matter cause the nigga fell with you this time." We all laughed.

"It's been an hour already? Key gon kill me." I zipped up my bag. "I have to take him a plate."

"Go ahead girl before he takes that ticket back."

I pulled up to Key's house around 8:45 PM. He was in the living room waiting for his hot home cooked meal that was now cold.

"I'm glad I didn't hold my breath," he pouted.

"Baby, you know I had to pack."

"We only going over there for a day."

"Do we have a hotel room?" He nodded yes. "Well, that's all that matters. I have to be prepared."

"That's why I love…" He stopped mid sentence and start fidgeting in the chair.

Was he about to tell me he love me and stopped?

He quickly changed the subject. "So, what did Mom cook?"

I began to unravel the aluminum foil. "Chicken, I think."

"I'm gonna to turn into a chicken pretty soon, all this chicken I've been eating."

"That should be interesting," I chuckled. "You can be my pet." He grabbed and laid a wet juicy kiss on my nose. *One in a Million* by Aaliyah sounded through the speakers. I began singing it to him. "Your love is a one in a million…it goes on and on and on…"

The doorbell rang and he went to answer it. I continued singing in the living room.

"What's up, Skyy?" Kenny greeted, walking straight upstairs with Key following. When they were privately tucked away in the bedroom, Kenny got down to business.

"Yo K man, that nigga Slim is talking." He sounded worried.

"Talkin' 'bout what?"

"What he gone do!"

"Well, what is that?" Key asked, studying Kenny's facial expressions.

"I don't know. I just heard he aint finished."

"I guess I got to watch my back." Key remained calm as can be.

Kenny tried passing him a 9mm gun. "Here, I brought you this just in case."

"You know I aint for all that. If the nigga won't fight me straight up, he's a bitch."

"You right, but just in case." Kenny tried to force the gun into his hand.

"I'm really not for this. I got too much to lose."

"It's too late now. You have something he wants, and he's not taking it too well."

"That's on him, she's mine now," Key expressed, arrogantly.

"Is this chick worth it?" Kenny shook his head forgetting he was the same one that assured Key to hold on while he can because good girls are hard to come by.

"Yo, don't come at me like that, Kenny."

He stared Key in the eyes hoping to get through to him. "Aint you the same one that told me she was a good one?"

He thought about it for a second, but kept on. "First, this was all about getting some. Now you acting like you all in love and shit."

"Kenny, it's time to roll," he stated, while opening the bedroom door.

"I'm not trying to be burying you, Key. I buried enough of my homies."

"Look, this aint none of your business. I can handle my own."

"Be careful, dawg. You're almost out of here."

They gave each other a pound and headed out the room. When Kenny walked down the steps, he gave me a hard stare. If looks could kill, I would have been a goner. Key let him out and came to sit beside me on the sofa.

"Here, I warmed your food up." I passed him the plate, but he just sat it on the table and looked at me. "Oh boy, what I do now?"

"Skyy, how do you feel about me?"

"What you mean?" I asked knowing it was time for the talk. I tried to hold my feelings for him in as long as I could, but from the look on his face it was time to let them all come pouring out.

"Exactly what I said. How do you feel?"

"I'm diggin' you a lot," I replied, hoping he would take it and leave it at that.

"So that's it? You just diggin' me?"

"Look Key, I'm not really ready to have this conversation with you. I don't know what you want me to say."

"Say how you feel. Damn, say something." He rose from the seat then sat right back down.

I felt the tears coming and Aaliyah's CD wasn't making it any better for me. "Key, I can't do this right now."

He leaned back on the sofa with a disgusted expression on his face. "Then leave, Skyy. Just leave!"

I went to get up and turned to him, eyes full of anguish. "I love you, okay? I love you." I broke down in tears.

He pulled me into his arms to console my weakened body. "Why you had to break me down like this, Key?"

"Why were you so afraid to tell me that you love me?"

I broke away from him and responded, "I'm tired of this. Tired of getting hurt, and always allowing myself to fall so easily."

He pulled me back into his space. "Skyy, you really don't have a clue, do you?"

"A clue about what? Me always being the fool in love?"

"No, about the feelings I have for you?" He gave a pregnant pause. "I love you too, Skyy."

I don't know if my heart stopped or skipped a couple beats, but I do know it sent a chill through my body. I didn't say anything after that. I couldn't. Just hearing the words I've been dying to hear for so long gave me an itch to cry harder.

We made love right there on the floor. The first time was good. All the times in between were lovely, but this time I couldn't even explain how it felt. The way he caressed me, held me in his arms, grabbed my butt and stroked through my hair felt different than ever before. All the times in the past I assumed I was in love, but it wasn't anything past lust. Now this was love, and never have I imagined it felt this way.

Please Lord, don't take this feeling away from me, I prayed as I gripped him tighter. He stroked in and out of my womb so gently. After that beautiful sexual encounter, we lay peacefully on the floor in each other's arms for the rest of the night.

"Skyy?" he whispered, running his fingers through the back of my hair.

I silently turned to look him directly in the eye.

"It wasn't supposed to turn out like this."

I agreed with the statement. "It never is."

Chapter 9

LIVING IT UP

We were up and out the house on our way to the Philadelphia International Airport by seven. The flight was scheduled to leave for Miami at eight-fifty. The airport had an unusual crowd and the lines were dreadful.

"Damn, where is everybody going?" asked Key, to the ticket agent.

"Sorry sir, there were a lot of delayed flights," the agent responded, apologizing for the crowd.

"My flight better be on time. I got things to handle."

She passed him the boarding passes with a belligerent smile. "Your flight will be boarding at 8:30, Sir. Enjoy!"

"If I wasn't mistaken, I would've thought you were flirting with her." I said, giving him a hard smack on the butt.

"Skyy, come on don't start."

"No, you don't make me pull out my can of whip ass."

He overlooked my jealousness. "Let's grab some breakfast before we board."

"No need for that Mr. Tyson. First Class serves breakfast," a stewardess advised, heading in the same direction.

"I know that, but I want some Mickey D's. Thanks anyway."

I eyed him suspiciously wondering how she new his name so well and asked, "Who was that babe?"

"I don't know, but I do remember her from my last flight."

"And she just remembers your name?"

"I can't help it if I'm a pimp."

"Pimp ya ass over here so I can keep an eye on you." I gripped his shirt pulling him in closer to me.

"I'm all yours, baby."

We landed in Miami International at eleven on the hour. When we got off the plane, there stood a gentleman dressed very professional down in the baggage claim area holding a sign that read Tykey Tyson. Key headed into his direction with a smile.

"Hey Mr. Tyson, let me get them bags for you," the man said, taking the bags.

Key instructed me to do the same. I didn't want to ask any questions, so I just went with the flow. He then guided us out to a black stretch limousine and held the door open for us to get in. The inside was decked out with a flat screen TV and a mini bar.

"So that's how ya'll do it out here?"

"I guess this is the life of a celebrity," he smiled.

"Calm down, you still a *r*ookie."

"Not for long."

We arrived at The Palms hotel in Miami Beach. As I walked through the lobby, I couldn't help but stare. It looked like nothing but royalty up in there. We took a tour out back to view the pool and it was breath taking. The junior suite we acquired was spacious and designed so beautifully like nothing I have ever seen before.

The next stop was the Arena. It was much bigger than it looked when watching a NBA game on television, and the scenery was stunning. When we went inside, the rest of the team was gathered on the gym floor talking to the coach. I saw a couple of other females on the sidelines gossiping and cutting their eyes in our direction.

I gave them the grizzly look right back and whispered to Key, "I hope they aint snobby."

"Girl, go over there and chill. I don't want to hear a peep out of you."

I walked over and to my surprise they were all friendly and down to earth. That was only because they were wives of the other players. After Key finished signing papers, the coach called for a celebration for the new rookie of the team, Tykey Tyson. The president of the team had a big brunch set up at some fancy hotel. It turned out to be the same hotel we checked into. Although they knew Key and I weren't married, I was still being referred to as Mrs. Tyson. I was living the life and enjoying every bit of it.

"Babe, I did have something to do in the morning back home, but we might stay over tonight."

"I didn't have anything planned," I advised, ready to pack up and move out here with him.

"Malone is having a party tonight. I told him we would be there."

"See, I knew I did some major packing for a reason."

"Did you bring that black dress I love?"

"You know I did. I got you, baby."

"That means I'll have to keep both eyes on you."

I recalled the line he used on me earlier and said, "I can't help it if I'm a pimp."

"Don't make me kill you, Skyy." We both laughed. "Come on to the room so we can handle our business first."

"Fine with me, Daddy."

We said our goodbyes and headed to the room for some real action. As soon as the door slammed shut, clothes were being ripped off from us both like we were mad men.

"Baby, wait before you pop my necklace."

He threw me back on the bed. "I'll buy you a new one."

"Oh, you wanna play rough?"

"You like it rough don't you?" he replied, ready to take our sex game to the next level.

"Yes, but can you handle it?"

"I can handle anything you got to give."

"Oh really?" I pulled him closer to me and said in a sexy voice, "Well, in that case, fuck me in my ass."

I was surprised he didn't fall out the way I felt his arms and legs go limp. "Are you serious?"

Again in a seductive way I said, "Fuck me in my ass, Key."

He gently spun me around and began to get himself wet with my juices. After a few more minutes of four play, he slid it in. I almost passed out. It was hurting so bad, but I could tell by the expressions on his face and the tone in his voice he loved it, so I didn't stop him. I tried not to dwell on the pain and concentrated on making him cum so he could get out of there. I threw the ass back making him go crazy out of his mind. After doing that, it didn't take too much longer before he had climaxed and was knocked out cold. I set the alarm clock so we wouldn't oversleep and went to get in the shower.

Damn that shit hurt, I thought as I brushed my teeth in the mirror. *I'm gonna kill Armani and Kizzy for talking me into doing it. If that's the way to get a nigga nose wide open, the hell with it.*

I comfortably placed myself into his arms after the hot shower drifting off not long after. I jumped up in the middle of my nap to gunshots realizing it was just a dream. I tried to catch my breath and envision what I just dreamt, but it was all a bluer. All I could recollect is hearing the gunshots. My stomach was feeling queasy, so I eased out of bed and ran into the bathroom. Soon as I hit the toilet I started throwing up non-stop. I sat crying on the floor because I knew what it was hitting for. Key didn't twitch one time, so I eased back down until the alarm clock went off forty-five minutes later.

"What time is it, Skyy?" he yawned.

"Nine o'clock." I hesitated a moment and thought about whether or not to tell him I might be pregnant.

"Let's get ready to roll out. I told them we'd be there around eleven."

"I have my stuff out and I ironed yours."

"Thanks babe. Come get in the shower with me."

After getting through round two, we were dressed and met the limo downstairs at quarter after eleven. "How are you Mr. Tyson?" asked the driver.

"I'm good," replied Key, looking fresh to death out of a Big & Tall magazine. He was laced with a funky white linen pants suite with white Gucci loafers to match. You would have thought his complexion was too dark for that, but no.

Not at all. It looked exquisite. It was so thin that the breeze revealed a little more than it should have.

"How about you pretty lady?"

"Fine, thank you."

"Are you going straight to the party, Sir?" he asked, opening the door for us. Key gave a head nod advising we were. "The ride is about twenty minutes."

When we arrived, there were people everywhere and cameras flashing. We stepped out the limo onto the red carpet. *This has got to be a dream*, I thought.

Key whispered, "You know how you are about pictures. Don't be making no crazy faces."

"Oh my God, it's Tykey Tyson," a female screamed out and all the females followed her pitch.

Damn, how is he getting all this attention and he's only a rookie? I know all these females didn't watch the draft. He pulled my arm up under his as we entered the building. It was decked out from top to bottom with different celebrities lounging all over.

"It's beautiful in here. Where are we?"

"This is Malone's vacation house. It's something like you aint never seen, huh?"

My facial expression said it all.

When Malone noticed us, he came over to greet us. "Wassup Tyson?" They gave the brotherly hug. "You look very nice, Skyy."

"Thank you," I blushed.

"Ya'll come in here and get some drinks." He escorted us to the pool area where one of the bars was located.

"Baby, I just want some wine. I don't really feel like that hard stuff."

"Okay, you can chill out here and I'll bring it to you." I took a seat and scoped out the rest of the place. When he brought the drinks back, I sat my glass down. "You okay? You don't look too good," he asked concerned.

"I'm fine. Let's dance."

We mingled around and watched as the rest of the guests came in. The party turned out to be really nice. It was about 2:30 A.M. when we headed back to our hotel. Key was so drunk he passed out without a word. I was glad because I wasn't ready to look him in his eye and tell him of the possibility of me being pregnant.

*****

It's been a couple days since the trip and I haven't been doing much but sleeping and throwing up anything that hit my tongue. I've also been avoiding Key and afraid to take a home pregnancy test. I was ignoring his calls, but it was just a matter of time before he would snap out about it.

"Mom, you're crazy," I said, laughing at what she'd just told me.

"What girl? I'm for real. Your mom still got it you know," she advised, doing the boxer shuffle around the living room.

"But Mom, a 20 year old guy tried to get your number?" I asked, confirming her statement.

"Yes! What's so hard to believe about that?"

"I'm a tell Dad to see what he thinks about it."

"Girl, don't make me get you," she snickered. "Why have you been up under me these last couple days anyway? What are you up to?"

"What you mean?" I played dumb. "I'm about to leave soon, so I'm trying to spend some time with you."

"My girl is heading off to college. I'm so happy for you."

"I'm happy too." I paused before continuing, "Mom," I paused again. "Never mind." She automatically assumed and questioned if there was something wrong between Key and I. "No, everything is good."

"Not too good I hope because you're getting out of here come September."

"I know, Mom."

I began to tell her how the trip went and how I got to meet the rest of the team and others at the party. She joked about her needing to be there when I told her how sexier they are in person. "See, that's exactly where I get it from."

"Whhhaaatt?" she griped.

"You're crazy. I'm going over Mashae's for a little while."

"I'm about to wash some clothes and make some laaasssaaaggna," she sang out the words of my favorite.

"Well, you know I'll be back."

I grabbed my keys and headed out the door. As soon as I pulled off, there was a car tailgating and high beaming me from behind. I disregarded whoever it was and kept going. The car sped up and blocked me from moving. *Who is this playing?* I thought, but should have known it was Slim. I shook my head in disbelief that he would take it this far.

As he jumped out to approach my car, I cracked the window slightly. "Slim why?" I asked, as he walked up.

"I tried to stop you. Get out for a minute so we can talk."

"No, what's up? You can talk through the window."

"Look Skyy, I ain't gon hurt you. You know I love you."

I was still skeptical. "If it's like that why don't you just let me be?"

"Just get out and talk to me for a minute and that's it. I'm done after that." I made sure I had my mace in my pocket before exiting the car. I didn't trust him that much. "What's up wit you? Why you doing this to me?"

"Doing what, Slim? We're not together no more."

"You're right, but can't we work it out."

"I tried to work it out wit you a number of times."

"I know, baby girl. But I got my act together now."

"How do you have your act together when you pull stunts like this?"

"I can't get your attention any other way. It seems like somebody got you occupied," he stated, bringing his tone a bit louder. I went to get back in the car but he stopped me. "Wait a minute! Just tell me if you're fuckin' that nigga."

"I'm not telling you anything. It's none of your business."

He put his hand around my throat so tight it felt like my eyes were going to pop out of my head. "What you mean it's none of my business?"

For that to be a busy street, it seemed like nobody took it that night. I tried to tell him I couldn't breathe, but his grip wouldn't allow me.

"Answer my question," he continued. "As a matter of fact, take a ride wit me." He reached in my window with his free hand and yanked the keys out of the ignition. "If you scream, I'll kill you," he warned.

Slim knew damn well I couldn't scream with the grip he had around my neck. I tried my best to fight him off, but it was useless. He threw me in his car and sped off. I began gasping for air. "Slim, please let me go. What are you doing?"

"I can show you better than I can tell you. Are you ready to tell me if you're fuckin' that nigga or what?"

"No, I'm not..." He backhanded me across my face before the lie could leave my tongue.

"You gon sit here and lie to me bitch." His eyes became a blood shot red and his complexion wasn't far from it. I knew I had to get the hell out of there quick. Suddenly, he started to unzip his pants. "I'll find out if somebody was up in there soon as I see how them walls feel inside."

I thought my ears were deceiving me. "What?!?" My heart was beating rapidly. I couldn't imagine what he was about to do to me, and I didn't want to pull the mace out just yet because I wouldn't be able to get him from that angle. He stopped and parked on a dead end alley way that had only one streetlight burning and three large green dumpsters at the end. There was a strong stench of urine and garbage mixed.

"Come here you whore," he demanded, leaning across the seat to grab me. I tried to swing and kicked him off. "I know you don't think you're stronger than me," he said, pulling my pants down. When he let me go to pull his pants down, I pulled the mace out and sprayed nonstop.

"What the fuck, Skyy. I can't see!" he yelled, struggling to get out the car.

I helped him out by kicking him in the ass and watched as he landed face down on the ground. I slammed the door and pulled off backing down the block without a second thought. I made it back to my car, and left his car there running with the keys and everything in it hoping a junkie or somebody would walk by and steal it. I called Mashae as I drove down the street soaked in grief and tears.

"Mashae, open the door. I'm turning the corner," I cried.

"Why are you crying, Skyy? What's wrong?" she asked, making her way to the door with the cordless phone.

"Just open the door." She stood outside waiting for me. Seconds later I was jumping out my car lividly. "I can't believe he tried to rape me. He tried to rape me," I explained, but she couldn't understand what I was saying.

"Stop crying. What are you saying? Who tried to rape you?" She helped me into the house.

"Slim!"

"Where is he?"

"I don't know. I left him somewhere?"

"Where Skyy?"

"I don't know…I don't know!" I screamed. She tried calming me down. "I don't believe this shit."

"Skyy, we have to report it."

"No! He's gonna get his, and not by the police." I went in the bathroom to get myself cleaned up. When I came out, I caught her hanging up the phone. "I know you aint call my mom."

"Why not? You have to tell her."

"I don't want my dad in this. I can't afford to lose him too. You know how Slim plays," I snapped at her.

"I didn't call your mom, I called Armani."

I knew Armani went straight to Q, and I wasn't ready for any more drama. Mashae kept trying to shove the phone in my face suggesting I call Key.

"No!" I said pushing it away. "I don't want him in this. I got him in enough. Why is this happening, Mashae? Why?" I broke down to the floor in tears. She came to hold me advising everything would be okay. "But it's not okay."

"Did he get a chance to do anything?" I didn't respond. "Skyy, what's the matter with you? Did he rape you or not?"

"I told you he didn't get a chance."

"Well, what's the matter? He's going to get what he got coming to him."

"I'm pregnant!"

"What, when, how?" she stuttered. "Did you tell Key?"

"No, and you don't either," I warned. My look was enough to express I meant what I said.

"You have to tell him, Skyy."

"Don't tell me what I have to do. I can't believe this shit is happening."

"Maybe you're not. Maybe your cycle is changing."

I give her credit for making it sound good, but she knew as well as I knew we both were in denial. She demanded we go get a test from the store. It took a while of badgering before I gave in. "What am I gonna tell my mom?"

"You just have to talk to her. We all make mistakes."

"This aint no mistake. It's just plain old stupidity."

"Stop crying before you make yourself sick."

"What if Slim spots my car out there? Come on, I have to go."

"Slim is not gon try nothing right now. He probably thinks you went straight to the police."

"I can't believe he did this to me. I use to love him and I thought he loved me."

"Love makes you do some crazy things. C'mon, let's go to the store."

We headed to the CVS on 20th & Oregon Ave. to get an EPT pregnancy test. Armani called informing she pulled up outside of Mashae's and would wait there for us to return. There she was waiting patiently but pissed.

"What did he do to you, Skyy?" I advised I was okay not wanting her blood pressure to go up. Every time she gets too excited we have to rush her to the hospital. "No it's not cool. That's it for that nigga. He got it coming," she said, pacing back and forth.

"What you do, Armani?"

"What? I aint do nothing," she lied.

I knew her too well to believe that. "Armani, what you do?"

"I just told my brothers. They said they tired of that nigga anyway. He was talking shit out in the streets about 'em. You know how that go," she said looking through the plastic bag in my hand. "What the hell? I know that aint..."

I stormed inside ready to get the facts over with. They pushed me upstairs eager for the results. "What are ya'll so hype for?"

"I'm about to be a God-Mom," teased Mashae.

"That baby gone have three God-Moms or none," Armani corrected her.

128

I grinned while stalling to go in the bathroom, but finally did. We waited a few minutes, and then Armani told me to go see. "No, you go see."

When she came out the bathroom she said, "Hey mommy." I snatched the test out her hand and she wasn't lying. I was going to be a mom, imagine that. "Time to call Key."

I threw the test on the floor. "No!"

"Why not? You have to tell him before he leaves."

"I don't know what I'm gonna do yet. I might not keep it. I can't believe I screwed up big time. My mom and dad gon be so disappointed in me."

"They'll get over it. You know I know cause I've been there," said Mashae.

"I suppose to go away to school. Now what am I gonna do and what am I gonna tell Key?"

"That he's gonna be a daddy."

"I know he's not ready for no kids."

"How you know? Did he say that?" They both asked at the same time.

"YEAH!"

"So why the hell ya'll wasn't strappin' up?" asked Armani, trying to make sense of the whole thing. I couldn't answer that. "He knew the consequences, so it's time to pay up."

It felt like the world was caving in on me. I began to feel dizzy and went to lay in Mashae's bed feeling sorry for myself. "Skyy, you can't just lay here and blame yourself. You have to go talk to him."

I ignored Mashae although she was right. I asked that they both leave me alone and close the door behind them. Involuntarily, they did.

Chapter 10

CONSEQUENCES AND REPERCUSSIONS

Armani came running up the steps to awake me. "Skyy, get up. Hurry! There was just a shooting on 22nd & Morris," she said, hysterically pulling me out the bed.

"Who got shot?" I asked, trying to get loose.

"I don't know. It said on the news that it was two men and a female."

I started slipping my pants on. "Did anybody die?"

"I don't know. Come on so we can go 'round there." She took flight back downstairs.

When we got to the block, the streets were packed. Everybody and their grandmamma were out trying to be nosy just like us. We wiggled our way through until finding someone we knew had the gossip.

"Meatball, what happened?" asked Mashae, trying to get the details from one of the local hustlers.

"Somebody shot Slim and DB. A female got shot in the crossfire, but I aint see who it was."

"Is he dead?" I came up out of nowhere waiting to hear the verdict.

"What's up, Skyy? Where you been?" he smiled.

"Is he dead?" I repeated edgily.

"Who Slim? Damn, ya'll was still messing around?"

I finally snapped at him. "Meat, what happened?"

"I'm not sure. They took them all out of here on stretchers."

Another guy named Shawn came up having more details. He informed us that a car full of guys drove by and started blasting at Slim and his friends, gunning one down.

"What about Slim? Is he dead or what?" I asked.

"I'm not for sure. Why you know him?" he asked trying to figure me out, but from the expression on my face he decided to continue the story. "The chick was over there arguing with them. I don't know if she had anything to do with it, but DB, Slim's homie, is the one that shot her."

After hearing that, I paused wondering where the hell Kizzy could be. I broke back to Mashae's house to call her paranoid as ever. "Skyy, what is it? Wait!"

They ran behind me screaming, but I kept truckin'. When they got to the house I was already dialing her number. "Who you calling?" asked Mashae, out of breathe.

"Where is Kizzy? Did ya'll talk to her today?"

"Yeah, I talked to her. She said she be over here later." A couple seconds later, it dawned on them what the guy just told us. "OH SHIT!"

"Where is she? Why she not answering the phone?"

"You think she went around there after I told her what happened to you?" Armani quizzed.

"Where the fuck is she?" I slammed the phone down now more worried.

"It probably wasn't her."

Less than a minute later a call came in on Armani's cell confirming our fears. Q had advised that it was Kizzy who got shot and to get down to the hospital. "Oh my God!" she exclaimed, but he advised it wasn't that serious for sure. She hung up the phone and jumped up. "Kizzy got shot! We have to go down to the hospital." We all panicked and ran to the car.

"Is she okay?" I asked crying.

"He said she is. We just have to go down there."

"She's not okay if she shot and in the hospital. I know Q aint do the shit while she was out there. What were they thinking?"

We drove in complete stillness to the hospital. The nurse told us that she was okay. After reviewing the report, she advised Kizzy tried to run when the shots rang out but one bullet caught her in the leg. Luckily it went straight through not causing too much damage. She also confirmed that one of the victims didn't make it out alive and the other was still in surgery, but didn't give their names.

"Can we see her?" We all were anxious.

"In a minute, the police is questioning her right now."

I circled around the waiting room wondering what Kizzy was in there saying. "Sit down Skyy, you're making me dizzy," said Mashae, staring at me nervously.

When the cops were done, they directed us in. "Kizz, what's the matter wit ya crazy ass?"

She placed a finger against her lips. "Why ya'll so loud?"

"What happened?" I was desperate to know what Slim said to her.

"I'll holla at ya'll when we get home." She nodded her head towards the door where detectives were still hanging around waiting for her to slip up. "I'm cool. It hurts like hell though."

"You a gun now. You done got shot," joked Mashae and we all laughed.

"You know I'm gonna strangle you, don't you?"

"Skyy, I could've shot him myself when Armani told me what he did to you."

"I'm just glad your crazy ass is okay." I mugged her. "Are they discharging you?"

"Yeah, I'm just waiting for my prescriptions."

"Is it hurting right now?" asked Armani, frowning her face at the blood seeping through the bandage.

"Nah, they gave me something, and whatever it was, that's what the prescription better be for."

We got out the hospital at a quarter to twelve. There was still no word on who made it and who didn't. Kizzy gave us the run down when we got home. She pulled up on Slim and jumped out to confront him about the attempted rape. He laughed in her face and said, "That bitch wanted it." Kizzy continued to badger him until she noticed a car slowly creeping down the block with its headlights off.

"I'm gonna kill Q. Why didn't he wait for you to get out of sight."

"I'm a kill him too cause he scared the shit out me, but I peeped them when they were riding up with the lights off. He gave me a signal to roll out, but DB saw him too. When I tried to run, he shot at me."

"Damn, I'm glad it was just your leg."

"Yeah, it could have been worse, but it wasn't so let's be thankful."

We all stayed at Mashae's house for the night hoping someone would call to tell us the latest. Instead, people just called to be nosy and find out what happened. Mashae pulled out some weed from her closet and two vanilla blunts. We never really smoked, but at a time like this, it was called for.

"I wonder if he made it," I said, as I took two puffs and passed it.

"If he did, it won't be for too long," Armani admitted, as she inhaled keeping up with the rotation.

"It's crazy out here. This is some movie type shit," said Kizzy. She was still coughing from the last puff she took two whole rounds ago. She was always the clown out the group when we smoked.

"He brought it all on his self."

That's the last thing that played in my head after Armani said it before I finally drifted off to sleep. In the middle of the night, I had another nightmare jumping up after hearing the guns shots, but everybody was still sleeping. This time I did more than just hear the shots. I felt them. I looked at my phone and saw that my voicemail was full. I knew it was Key, but didn't bother to check any. I've been avoiding him all day trying to figure out a way to give him the news. I don't know why I was so scared, but I was. Maybe it was because I didn't want him to take his love away. Babies always seem to drive guys away. I knew I had to tell him and I would sooner or later. But that night just wasn't the right time.

*****

It was now August 5th, Samir's 18th birthday. Him and I use to sit and talk about how this day would feel. For him to not be around was truly painful for me. I'm sure he would have been granted a full scholarship to any 1st division college with his football skills being this was his last year at Southern high school. Everyday we take for granted our precious lives not knowing what could be in store the following day. I just wish I'd got to say goodbye before he was taken away.

My parents and I were down at the grave sight placing flowers on the tombstone. We also released some *I Miss U* balloons into the air in remembrance of him. I imagined Samir taking them all into his arms and popping each one like he did when we were kids. "I miss you, Mir. I miss you so much," I smiled. "Maybe if you were here, I wouldn't be getting into so much trouble. You know you were always on my back. I love you, baby boy. Don't ever forget that." I touched the tombstone and walked away.

"You alright, Skyy?" My dad questioned, as I wiped tears from my face.

"I'm okay, Dad. I feel a lot better now."

On the way home, I watched my cell read Key's number several times before I decided to stop avoiding the calls. My voice sounded stressed, aggravated and emotional all in one, but he held back all sympathy if any was there.

"You aint get any of my messages?"

"I got them, but I can't talk right now. I'll call you when I get home," I advised, trying to cut the conversation short because of my parents.

He went on not letting me hang up that easily. "What you call yourself ducking me or something?"

I remained humble. "No Tykey! I said I'd call you back."

"Now you calling me by my full name. What's up with you? You don't want to be bothered anymore?"

"I have to talk to you, but not right now."

"Say what you gotta say. You want me to stop calling?" I answered with silence. "Skyy, just say it and I'm gone."

"Can I please call you back? I'm just leaving the cemetery."

"Yeah, you do that cause I'm tired of playing these mind games witchu."

I heard him throw the phone down, which didn't end the call because I could still hear him tossing things around in the background. I hesitated to close the flap to my phone knowing it was just a matter of time before my mom started to question me.

"Is something going on with you and Key?"

That's exactly why I didn't want to talk to him now, I thought before responding "No, Mom."

"Well, what's going on?"

"Nothing! Just let it go."

"Who you think you talking to?"

"I'm just saying I don't feel like talking about it right now." I tried to make it sound short and sweet.

"He seems like a nice guy, Skyy..." She just went on and on, but I wasn't listening. I was in my own world daydreaming about Key's reactions when he hears he's going to be a father. "You hear me, Skyy?"

"Yes Mom, I hear you." I continued to stare out the window planning how to play out tonight. I thought of different ways to tell Key I was pregnant, but I knew came time to tell him, my mind would go blank.

When we arrived home, there were a couple of messages on my answering machine. One was from Mashae telling me how she bumped into Key and explained to him that I was going through some changes. The other was from Slim. As soon as I heard his voice, I froze up and saved it because I had more important things on my mind. The phone rang interrupting my daze.

It was Key sounding like he'd lost every bit of patience he had. "I thought you said you were gon call me when you got home?"

"Key, I just walked in the door. Give me a break."

"Skyy, tell me what the deal is so I can do me."

I was pissed after hearing that. "What you mean do you?"

"Exactly what I said."

"It's like that now?" I asked, wondering where all this was coming from.

"That's how you're making it. Is this how you want it?"

"I'll be over there so we can talk in person. Is that okay with you?"

"Hurry up cause I have something to do."

I couldn't believe he was talking to me like that. "I'll be over there in a minute." This time I slammed the phone down because he was really acting like a nut. "Mom, I'll be back in a little while," I advised, charging down the stairs.

"Okay, bring me back some cigarettes."

"I really don't know how long I'm going to be."

"Just bring them when you come."

I stopped and looked at her on the way out. "Okay, I love you." I needed her to feel my pain without knowing I was hurting.

"I love you too. Be careful."

I stood there and watched as she walked up the steps thinking about how I was going to tell her that I had let her down. Two tears trickled down my cheekbone as I continued on out the door.

Key was sitting on the outside stairs waiting for me when I pulled up. "Why you out here waiting for me? It's not that deep." I walked pass him inviting myself into the house.

"I want to know what's going on. So, what's up?" he said, standing in place on the front steps. I demanded he come inside but he wouldn't. "Skyy look, I'm not playing games with you. What's up?" I gave nothing but dead air. "You hear me talking to you, girl?"

I turned around. "Who the hell you think you talking to, Key? I'm not one of them chicken heads you use to messing with."

"I don't care who you are. You been avoiding me for almost a week now and you questioning why I'm acting like this? You always want to use that *I'm going through a phase* shit as an excuse, but it aint working this time."

"It's not an excuse. You don't even know the half of it."

"I know you're not mad cause your boy got shot," he stated, giving me an uncertain look.

"Aint nobody worried about Slim." He hunched his shoulders looking relieved. "Look," I paused and went to sit on the sofa. He followed. "Why do you have to be so hard all the time?"

"I wanna know what's going on. If you wanna call it quits, say it and it's over."

I started getting emotional just thinking about losing him. "Just like that? It was fun while it lasted, huh?"

"I'm not gonna be chasing after you like you the shit or something. I got too much going on around me."

"Who you think you are? I don't care about what you got or about to get. I guess now you wanna clown on me cause you think I'm playin' you."

"That doesn't even matter. All I'm saying is tell me so you don't get your feelings hurt."

I sat staring at this guy I thought was so sweet and sentimental. The same guy I was just boo-loving with. Now he done flipped the script and showed his true colors.

"Don't just sit here quiet and shit. Talk! You wanted to talk, right?"

"You know what, Tykey? Fuck you!" I went to walk out the door, but he grabbed me.

"Fuck me? No fuck..." I smacked him before he could get it all out. He grabbed my arms real tight and started shaking me irrationally. "Don't you ever put your hands on me. I will kill you."

I tensed up and out of rage screamed out, "I'm pregnant!"

"You what?" he queried, freeing his manly grip. "By who?"

I whaled on him uncontrollably for having the nerve to come out his mouth like that. How do niggas even have the audacity to ask that question knowing the answer? "What you mean by who? You aint shit, Tykey."

He threw me down on the sofa and started pacing back and forth. "Nah...Nah...You lying. I'm not having no babies."

"But you can cum all up in me. Now you aint having no babies?"

"I'm not having no babies," he yelled, then lowered his tone. "I got too much going on right now."

"You should've thought about that before you was sticking it raw."

"You should've been on the pill or something."

The typical nigga is quick to blame the female. "No, you should've been prepared," I explained. "You never even asked to began with."

"How much money does it cost?"

"Does what cost?"

"An abortion," he bluntly snarled.

"What you mean? I didn't say I was getting an abortion."

"I know you aint thinking 'bout keeping it. You can't stick me with no baby cause I'm not having it."

"You aint got to do shit for me or my baby. You think I need you?

"You tryna stick me aint you?" he smirked.

"Aint nobody tryna stick you. You aint that serious, *N*igga," I yelled. "How can you do me like this?"

"Do you like this? Look how you doing me!"

He tried to place the blame my way, but I wasn't having it because I can't make a baby on my own. Without his little tadpoles there would be no baby. Momma always told me it takes two to tangle and she never told me nothing wrong.

"What you tryna say I set you up?" I got up to leave. "I can't believe you actually think that."

"Where you going? We aint done talkin'."

"I'm done!"

He grabbed me back. "No we're not! What you gon do?"

"I don't know," I screeched with my lips barely moving.

"It seems like you had more than enough time to think about it. Is that why you were avoiding me? Who else knows about this?" he asked, wondering if he's the first.

"Armani, Kizzy and Mashae," I answered, in a low tone and he snapped.

"Damn, you told them before you told me?" I cooled him down by advising they were there when I took the test. "Why didn't you call me then?"

"Cause I knew you were gonna act like a dickhead. Just like you doing now." I crushed his pride after that comment. "Why this got to be about you? What about me and what I want?"

"You want to go to school."

"And this won't stop me," I assured him. "I'm going to raise my child with or *without* you."

"Now your talking like you done made up your mind."

I grabbed my head and sat back down frustrated with disgust. "I don't know, Key. I just don't know."

He was still being so cruel. "Think of something! Matter of fact, I'll help you. We should make an appointment to go see the doctor to handle this today."

"You are so inconsiderate. How can you be this cold?"

"Cold? I'm thinking about my future," he paused for a moment. "And yours."

"No, you're thinking about yourself like you always do. You aint never gon have nothing as long as you keep treating people like this. I thought you were so different, but I'm glad

142

the true you came out." I proceeded out. "I'll call you and let you know what my decision is."

I slammed the door and left him standing with a blank expression on his face. I went straight home, but sat in the car a while to get my thoughts together. What did I do to deserve this? What did I do that was so wrong? I cried and cried and cried. It began to get dark so I went in the house hoping my mom was upstairs, but wasn't that lucky. She heard me close the door and yelled out for me from the kitchen.

I crept upstairs before hand. "A'ight, I have to go to the bathroom first." I knew she would notice my eyes being red, so I tried to wash them with cold water but it didn't help much.

"Skkkyyy," she called out rushing me. I stalled. "Come here!" I went down to get it over with. "Why you didn't tell me that boy got shot?"

I knew whom she was talking about but still asked, "Who?" I had the refrigerator door open like I was looking for something.

"You know who, Slim. Who did it?" she asked, wondering if I had anything to do with it.

"I don't know, Mom."

"Well, you went around there after it happened."

"Dang, do people run back and tell you everything?" I asked, sucking my teeth.

"Why didn't you tell me? That's why I'm so glad you don't deal with him anymore. That's exactly why!" She went on giving the third degree lectures at the wrong time.

"Mom, I'm going upstairs to lay down."

"What's the matter?" she questioned, looking in my eyes. "It's only nine o'clock." She walked closer to me examining my face with her hands. "What are you crying about?"

I couldn't hold them back any longer. Tears suddenly soaked my whole face. "Please just let me go get some rest."

"Did somebody do something to you?" I didn't respond so she took me into her arms. "Skyy, tell me."

"Nobody did nothing to me, I messed up. You're gonna be so mad at me."

"It can't be that bad. What happened, baby?" A light bulb must have gone off inside her head. "Oh no, Skyy. You're pregnant?"

Why do parents always have to know, I thought. "Yes, I messed up so bad."

She hugged tighter. "Stop crying. Goodness Skyy, why weren't ya'll using protection?"

"Mom, I was so stupid. I'm so sorry."

"Stop crying and go get yourself together before your dad walks in. I'll be up to talk to you."

I heard my mom through the vent crying to my grandma on the phone when I reached my room. That made me feel more guilt and hurt than I already had. I felt like crawling in a hole and never coming out. My mom never came to talk to me that night because she too had to get herself together. I sat in the middle of my bed in an Indian style position looking at old pictures. I reminisced about the old days when everything was good and everybody was happy. "I need you right now, Samir. Please help me."

I turned the other way toward the phone thinking about the messages Slim left and the last one I never listened to. I leaped up and played all three. The automatic voice recording said:

You have three saved messages. First saved message, June 18th, *"Shorty, you think it's over but it's not."* He laughed. *"How ya cousin doin'? Did he die? I'll see you sooner than later. Peace!"* Slim sounded so hard it made my skin crawl. The machine continued.

Second saved message, July 5th, *"Shhooorrrrtttty, where you at? I was waiting for you. Didn't I say it aint over? Huh? Betta get it right or else! I aint got to even go there cause you know what I'm saying, right?"* He laughed before hanging up. I couldn't figure out why this was so funny to him. This was my life he was violating.

Third saved message, August 5th, the one I never listened to. *"That's it, I said it aint over. I guess I can show you better than I can tell you. You fuck'n whore. You know I like to finish what I start. BANG!"* was the sound at the end.

The vibration of him slamming the phone down startled me. I saved all three messages and listened to the machine say "there are no more messages" a few times hoping it was one more from him apologizing for acting like that. But there was nothing more he had to say.

I laid back down with my head spinning. I tried to go to sleep but couldn't, so I went downstairs when I heard my mom and dad go up to their room. I stayed up watching TV half the night until I fell asleep on the sofa. The next morning, I awoke from the footsteps of my father coming down the stairs.

"Skyy, what you doing down here?" he asked, on his way out to work.

"I couldn't sleep last night so I came down here."

"Is something bothering you?"

145

"No Daddy, I'm okay."

"Come talk to me if you need to." I wanted to tell him so bad, but I couldn't push myself to do it. I hugged him so tight not wanting to let go. "Boy, it's been a while since I got one of these hugs. Maybe you shouldn't be able to sleep more often," he grinned. "I'm going to work, so call me there if you need me. I love you, Skittles."

That was my nickname he had given me as a child. When I heard his truck pull out the driveway, I took the blanket and went back up to my room. A little while later I heard some more footsteps coming down the hall. I took a deep breath preparing myself for a speech.

"I'm cooking some breakfast. You want some?" my mom asked, looking like she didn't get that much sleep either.

"A little I guess," I mumbled, trying to make out her attitude.

"I'm putting it on now so come on." I took a minute to go down because I knew it was time to talk. She didn't even wait for me to step both feet into the kitchen before asking, "So what are you gonna do?" I shrugged my shoulders. "You can't sit around all depressed. What's done is done."

"Mom, no lectures. Please!"

"Lecture! It's time for you to start acting mature. This is your life Skyy, and it's up to you to take control. How far are you?"

My look alone advised I wasn't sure because I haven't been to see a doctor. It took me forever to get up enough nerve just to take an over the counter test.

"Girl, get on the phone and make an appointment. This is nothing to be playing with."

"I know, but I wasn't sure what I was gonna do."

"So what! You still should go see a doctor to make sure everything is okay. You weren't using protection. Who knows what else you may have." I looked up at her. "Don't look at me like that. What? You think you can't catch these diseases being passed around here? You don't know who else that boy been screwing."

"Just the other day you were saying how much you like him. Now cause I'm pregnant you're mad at him."

"I do like him. He's a respectful young man."

I was tempted to say, *that's what you think,* but I kept quiet.

"I'm disappointed with the both of you. It takes two to make a baby. Where is he anyway? He needs to come over here so we can all talk about what's going to be done. How does he feel about it?"

I couldn't bear to tell her how he treated me last night, so I told the half-truth. "He said neither of us is ready for a baby."

"And he's so right. What are you gon do about school?"

"If I have this baby I'll still go to school."

"It will be very hard, Skyy. It's not as easy as you may think. And how will ya'll work this out with him living in a different state?"

"I don't know. We haven't talked about it yet."

"What are ya'll waiting for?" I didn't respond. "I'm not sitting around here with no babies. I'm not ready to settle down in the house and play fulltime grandma." She took a long deep breathe before continuing. "Well, you have to tell your father cause I'm not saying anything."

My dad? How was I going to break it down to him? I started crying as soon as she said that. "Don't cry now. You better save them tears so he can feel sorry for you instead of ringing your neck."

"Mom, how could I be so stupid?"

She walked around the island in the middle of the floor to hug me. "Skyy, you're not stupid. Shit happens! We all make mistakes, but we just have to make sure we learn from them. When you make the same mistake twice, then it's considered stupid. I could have strangled you last night. That's why I waited until today to talk to you."

"I heard you through the vent in my room on the phone crying."

"I was talking to Momma. She helped me feel a little better. Even though she rubbed it in my face that I made the same mistake when I was your age. I lost the baby at three months into the pregnancy."

"By Dad?" I asked and she confirmed it was. This was the first I heard of it, and could tell by the look in her eyes she was still hurting after all these years. "How did he feel?"

"He was upset, but I just told him everything happens for a reason. That's when we got our finances together and two years later, you came."

"Maybe if I have a boy I can name him after Samir."

"If he was here, you know him and your father would be hounding you right now. I know he is turning in his grave."

"Yeah I know, but I wish he was here."

"I do too Skyy, but he's in our hearts. That's where he'll be from now on." She gave me another hug and kiss. "I'm about to make a few runs. Wash them dishes for me. I'll be back in a little while."

I did as I was told and washed the dishes. Afterwards, I comfortably balled up on the sofa and watched TV, mostly the baby channel. I really didn't feel like doing much, so I layed low in the house the rest of the day hoping for no disturbance. I haven't heard from Key all day and it was hard to think about living without him. He probably figured it was all on me. Him being on his way across the map to make some major cheese doing what he loved to do was a blessing. I guess nothing was gonna stop that, not even his own blood.

Chapter 11

LOVING HIM

A couple hours later, I got a surprise visit from Kizzy. When I heard the knock at the door, I got up to go answer it glad to see her, given that I haven't been out with the girls lately. The state of depression I endured the last couple days really took a toll over me. I wasn't eating, sleeping, and barely had the strength to wash at times. Aside from the depression, the morning sickness was breaking me off badly.

"What you want Kizzy?" I kneeled down to kiss her son. "Hey Mookie."

"Why the hell you got your phone off?" she asked, pushing pass me.

"Cause I don't feel like being bothered."

She started limping back towards the door with her cane looking like somebody's grandmother. "A'ight, bye then!"

"Sike, girl." I pulled her back inside.

"Why you been in the house?" I explained that I haven't been feeling up to par lately with everything going on.

She caught me up on what I'd been missing, which wasn't much besides the fact that the streets were talking. Mainly about the shootings and giving off many different stories of what went down with Slim. Then a big grin came upon her face before advising she'd recently saw Key.

"So," I responded, in a nasty tone. "He cut up when I told him I was pregnant. Acted just like I thought he would."

Kizzy couldn't believe the story I had to tell and couldn't wait to run into him again to tell him about himself. I didn't even want to give him the satisfaction of knowing how bad he'd hurt me, so I demanded she keep it quiet. She also got a little worried when I told her my mind was made up about keeping the baby. Everyone knew how strict my parents were, and for them to find out that their baby girl is about to have a baby was a whole 'nother story.

"Did you tell your mom?"

"Yup!" She stood up from the seat portraying like she was about the fly out the door assuming my mom hit the roof. "Actually, she took it better than I expected."

"That's how it always is. What about your dad?"

"He doesn't know yet. She said I have to tell him myself."

"Don't want to be around for that one, for sure." I mugged her out my way for being a punk. "Skyy's about to be somebody's mother. Who would have ever thought?"

"Not me, that's for sure."

"Well, at least we know the bratt will be taken care of," she said, referring to Key's career.

Again I tried to explain Key's and my position. I'm not banking on him, especially after the way he treated me thinking I planned all this. If he doesn't want any kids now or ever, that's on him. Like I said, I'll take care of this child with or without him, and you can put your money on that.

"I wish I could have been a fly on that wall," she chuckled.

"You are so nosy. What side of the family does it come from?"

Monica's video *Before you walk out my life* came on BET and Kizzy started singing it. "Never meant to cause you no pain…I just want to go back to being the same. I only wanna make things right…before you walk out my life…" She swayed back and forth with her son on her lap, looked over at me grinning and said, "You better call him up and sing this to him girl."

"I'm not worrying about Key. Let him keep it movin' if that's what he wanna do."

"Whatever girl, you know you want ya baby daddy by your side."

"I want a husband. I promised myself all through high school I wasn't going to be nobody's baby mama. Look at me now."

"Too late for that. You better grab ya man and stop playing."

"What am I suppose to do? He don't want the baby, so therefore he doesn't want me."

"I just think you caught him off guard."

"Off guard! Instead of acting like an asshole, he should have been asking me was I cool. Did I need anything? Was I hungry? How many weeks am I? He didn't ask any of those questions like a real dude suppose to. He just started acting like a park ape."

"That's niggas for you. He'll come around, Skyy. You just have to give him some time."

"Time? I hope it's not too late by then. I'm not waiting around for him to wanna play house and be a family. I got needs too. You know?"

"That's when a nigga starts acting right. As soon as they see you with somebody else doing what they suppose to be doing." She finally confessed. "I knew what was going on already. I just wanted to hear your side of the story."

"What he do go running to Kenny?"

"More like crying to Kenny." That was hard to believe because Key swears he's so tough. "I'm serious," she said, with a sly grin. But it was still hard for me to believe Kenny would snitch on his man like that.

"Kenny was pissed off at you until I put him in his place. He thought you were just after his money until I knocked some sense in him."

"That's why he gave me that dirty look the other night over at Key's house. I was wondering why he came back downstairs questioning how I felt about him."

"That's what everybody thinks, but they don't know how you feel inside."

"You right, but I don't care cause if I could get a nickel for how much pain I'm going through right now, I'd be rich."

"You mean we'd be rich. Don't forget who was there to take all of your shit," she said, recalling all the stuff I put her through growing up. "Get up and stop moping around feeling sorry for yourself." She reached for the phone on the table. "This calls for a waiting to exhale session. Time to round up the girls. Take me home to drop my son off."

"To who? Don't tell me Tyrik is back," I frowned, hoping she didn't give in that soon.

"Hell no! Rosie is there."

When we got to Kizzy's house, Armani and Mashae were pulling up at the same time. "I don't know what ya'll whores is dress for. I'm not going out," I stated, getting out the car.

They knew me better than that. I wasn't going to spend another day in the house alone being miserable and helpless. Kizzy convinced me to go with them down to the *M Lounge* on 2nd & Chestnut Street for Karaoke night. This wasn't a rowdy spot and the food was good, so it didn't take much convincing. I hurried home to change my attire happy to be swinging out with my girls again.

After hopping out the shower, I wrapped a towel around me and began to brush my teeth. I examined my face in the mirror noticing a little glow. A smile appeared across my face as I rubbed the tiny pudge in my stomach before exiting the steam filled room.

I heard my father coming down the hall towards my room, so I hurried and threw on my black Capri's and a tank top. "Where is your mom, Skyy?" he asked, knocking before entering.

" I don't know. She said she was going to the store."

"She's not answering her cell phone."

"Try Aunt Shena's house cause I think she was stopping by there."

"Oh okay. Do you have something you want to talk to me about?"

My heart dropped. "Why would you ask that, Dad?"

"Just asking," he lied. My mom had warned him that we needed to talk about a few things, but she didn't say what.

"I do, but can I talk to you about it later?"

"Whenever you're ready, I'll be here."

"Okay." I gave him a kiss and headed downstairs. The phone was ringing in my bedroom, but I heard Armani beeping the horn so I nixed it and went out the door.

Old City was filled with heavy traffic. This was a downtown area in the city with a variety of places to eat and drink. *The M Lounge* was a known spot to chill and get your drink on. Too bad I could only do one of the above. Fortunately, we found some seats and sat down.

"You getting up there tonight, Mashae?" I giggled. The last time we came she sang *I believe I can fly* by R. Kelly embarrassing the hell out of us.

"I don't believe ya'll let me get up there and embarrass myself like that."

"You believed you could fly, so you wanted to sing the song to let everyone else know."

One of the waitresses approached our booth. "Can I get you ladies anything to eat or drink?"

They all ordered drinks, but I ordered food. Key snuck up behind me out of nowhere and whispered, "Waazzup?" in my ear hitting a nerve.

"Why you always have to do that shit, Key? Damn!"

"My bad. I didn't mean to scare you." He was smiling like nothing was wrong. "I came over here to see you since you haven't returned any of my messages."

"I didn't get any messages," I lied as if I checked. I was also wondering how he knew I would be there. "If you really wanted me, you would have found me like you always do. I decided not to block your number out just in case you stopped acting like a dickhead."

"That's how it is now?"

"You made it like that. I'm not about to discuss this situation with you here."

"I was told to meet you here."

I turned to look at Kizzy. She dropped her head down telling on herself. I kicked her under the table disregarding Key's request for me to take a walk to talk. "I said I'm not discussing this here with you, so holla at me later." I turned my back to him.

"Damn! Just give me a second to talk to you. Why you always have to be like that?"

"Cause I don't feel like talking to you. When I tried to talk, you weren't trying to hear what I had to say."

"I'm sorry," he emphasized, hoping I would just brush it under the rug.

"Yeah you are," I implied.

He was so persistent. "I guess I deserved that. So can I holla at you real quick?"

Mashae was pinching my leg under the table, and Armani suggested they go and pick out a song for her to destroy tonight. I gave them all an evil look as they got up and he sat down. "I didn't ask you to sit down. What do you have to say?"

"How are you feeling?"

"Oh, You care now? How considerate."

"Skyy, if you give me a chance to apologize for acting a fool, I will." He grabbed my hand unto his. "Stop giving me this shitty ass attitude."

I was still in so much pain that I didn't know how to express anything but attitude. Although seeing him brought me some joy, I couldn't forget how he treated me just the other day. "How do I suppose to feel, Key?"

"I'm sorry, Skyy. You just struck that on me and I didn't know how to react. Look, I'm not gon mess up your night.

Just come over tomorrow so we can talk and get everything situated."

"If I have time."

He looked down slightly shaking his head and biting on his bottom lip to keep his cool. "Are you going to come or not?"

I wanted him to explode. I was waiting for a reason to smack him again. "I'll call you before I come, if I choose to."

"I'll talk to you tomorrow, a'ight?" I rolled my eyes. "Skyy, tomorrow okay?" he ordered, in a threatening tone.

Those were his last words before departing from the table. He looked as if I should be the one feeling sorry for him. I went to find the girls so I could express myself. "What the hell ya'll tell him to come here for?"

"Ya'll needed to talk," said Kizzy.

"It's not your place to…."

Mashae cut the conversation short by grabbing us all to the dance floor. I slipped away and went to sit back down. It felt like somebody was watching me like a hawk for the rest of the night. I'm pretty sure it was Key in the corner somewhere inspecting my every move.

"Damn, did you see that nigga all on me like that?" grinned Armani, as they came back to the table.

I watched as they all stumbled into their seats. "Ya'll better calm down before ya'll pass out."

"I'm toasted and ready to sing," Mashae admitted.

Just then the DJ asked everybody to clear the floor. It was time to act a fool. "What you singing tonight, girl?"

"I'm not cutting up tonight. I'm not drunk enough."

Kizzy passed her a shot glass filled with tequila. "Well here, take this shot cause I need a good laugh."

After a few people went, Mashae decided to go. She sang *Weak* by SWV. At the end of the song, I noticed Key going up there to get on the mic. "I know he is not about to try to sing," I blurted, covering my mouth.

"Come on Armani. I got to get a close up for this one," said Kizzy, pulling Armani from her chair.

I slouched down in my seat as they left me alone. I could see Mashae talking to him before the others reached that section. *He's about to embarrass me. I know he is. Shit! I'm about to roll out. Then again, I know he wouldn't do that. Would he?* I thought over and over in my head.

The girls came back to the table grinning from ear to ear like they'd just hit jackpot. "What he doing?" I asked, anxiously waiting for an answer.

"He's just about to act a fool. Why are you sweating?" Kizzy wiped my forehead with her napkin.

When I heard the beat to the song come on my mouth fell open. "Oh my God! He's not about to do this."

It was *If I Could Turn Back The Hands Of Time* by R. Kelly. My eyes instantly swelled with tears as the words softly rolled off his tongue. "How did I ever let you slip away...never knowing I would be singing this song someday...and now I'm sinking, sinking to rise no more...ever since you closed the door..." My stomach was turning in knots and filled with butterflies moving in a circular motion. When he finished and the song died out, I was in tears.

"Girl, get yourself together," whispered Kizzy, smacking my leg.

"Damn! He almost had me in tears," Armani added.

I looked around the club and it looked like he had everyone ready to go home and make up. "Walk me to the bathroom, Kizzy."

On the way to the restroom area, Key was leaving off the dance floor. Our eyes met and we watched one another until we couldn't anymore. "I don't believe he sang that song like that. He's crazy," I commented, while wiping my face and fixing my hair.

"I can't wait to clown him about it," Kizzy giggled, still tickled.

"I'm still not messing with him."

"Girl, come on. I'm not trying to hear this nonsense. I'm ready for another drink."

Key's homies were in their section playfully throwing hits at him. "Look, they on his head. Did you tell him to sing that, Mashae?"

"No! I was trying to talk him out of it."

I sat thinking about what he wanted to say to me tomorrow. Was this song the first step to some sort of apology? I was desperate to know and ready for the sun to rise. "Ya'll ready to roll out?"

"Hold up! Let me go give this dude my number," said Armani.

"What dude?" I frowned, glancing over at Rome.

"The one I was dancing with. I told him I'd be back."

"Do you see Rome over there? He's gonna kill you."

"We already agreed we just gon be friends. I told him I need space to maneuver." She swaggered away.

How could you not admire her game? She came back after they had exchanged numbers. I spotted Rome staring

159

out the corner of his eye, but she didn't care. "Here we go. More drama."

"Please, I'm drama free," she advised.

As good as that may have sounded, the future would for sure tell us otherwise…

When I got home, I went straight to sleep wondering whether or not to make that call tomorrow. I should've known he would be the one calling me bright and early.

The following morning, I answered still half asleep. "You still sleep, Shorty?" Key sounded wide awoke and knew he had it coming.

"What you think?" I replied, with an attitude.

"What time you coming over here?"

"Key, I told you I would call you. Did you forget?"

"No, but I was hoping you would be glad to hear from me after what I did for you last night."

I was cracking up inside. "You aint do that for me."

"You know I was singing to you. Stop front'n."

"I'll call you when I get up," I said, breaking the conversation, but he tried to keep it going. "I said I would call…"

He cut me off. "All right…All right…Call me soon as you brush ya teeth cause I know ya breath is humm'n."

I hung up excited to hear the sound of his voice ring in my ears. I had to laugh because he had some nerve talking about somebody's breath stink the way his smell in the morning. The aroma of some good morning cooking hit my nose so I put some clothes on and followed the smell.

"Hey Mom," I greeted, entering the kitchen. She gave me a kiss and continued on frying bacon. "Where's Daddy?"

"He went to work today for a couple of hours." She softly smacked my hands as I snatched a piece of bacon off the table. "I didn't make that for you. Fry your own, and when do you plan to talk to your father? You prolonged long enough."

"I'll talk to him tonight."

"What are you waiting for?" I knew she had already given him a heads up that I needed to speak with him, so I suggested she finish the job. "I'm not telling him anything. That's your job."

I snatched another piece of bacon and went back upstairs.

"What am I going to put on today? Got to wear something sexy so he can beg for some. Then I can tell him no," I giggled, dancing around the room.

After getting dressed, I called Key. He answered the phone out of breath, but I didn't bother to ask him why. "The door will be unlocked," he informed.

"So, I got the key," I uttered before hanging up in his ear.

When I walked in, I sat on the sofa not acknowledging my presence. Five minutes later, he came down the steps and smiled. "When were you gonna tell me you were here?"

I loved the attitude I've been giving, so I kept it going. "You see me now, don't you?"

He sat beside me. "Skyy, let's cut the crap now. We're gonna have a serious talk. All the bullshit is pushed to the side." He sat upright with his arms behind his head. "How are you feeling? Are you hungry?"

161

"I didn't come over here to get pampered. What's the deal?"

He shrugged his shoulders feeling optimistic. "This is the deal. As a matter of fact, answer this. Are you keeping the baby?"

"What do you want?" I asked, hoping he had a change of heart.

"It doesn't matter what I want cause you're gonna do what you want anyway. Did you make a decision or not?" he snapped.

"I'm keeping my baby, and that's that."

He put his head down for a second, then back up to me. "That's what I want, Skyy."

"What? What do you mean that's what you want?" I stumbled over the words expecting to hear something else.

"You heard me. That's what I want. I want to be a big part of this child's life."

I wanted to say *talk about a change of heart,* but held in the sarcasm. "What changed your mind?"

"Let's just say I got to thinking about more than myself." Automatically, I assumed his mother or someone else talked him into this new decision, which made him offended. "Nobody can't talk me into wanting a baby. What's the matter with you?"

"I'm saying, first you're screaming in my face, then your singing *If you could turn back the hands of time.*" Neither of us could hold in our laugh after flashing back on last night.

"So what's up, Key? What are you really saying?" I asked, needing to understand exactly what he wanted.

"I'm saying we're gonna have this baby, and I'm gonna handle my responsibilities."

After that being said, it was now time to work out some kind of living arrangements and transportation to and from Miami. I can see me now riding up and down the road or on US Airways like it's my second home. The one thing I won't let this whole ordeal conflict with is school. I was determined to get through this all one way or another.

"I'm still going to school. I'm not gonna let this stop me. And I'll find a job too so I will have a head start on a few things."

"Nah Shorty, I can't have that," he said, gently rubbing my thigh.

"Have what? Me not going to school isn't an option."

"I'm not saying that, but I can't have you working while you're pregnant. Now that's not an option."

"Look at you trying to run things already. You can stop that right now."

"Aint nobody trying to run you." He took a deep breath. "Listen, I want you to move to Miami with me. You can go to school out there."

I had a confused expression on my face. "Huh?!?"

"I'm not going to live without my boy, but I'm not gonna let him put my career on hold either."

"Live without your boy?" I reiterated, with my hand on my hip.

"Oh, you too," he chuckled.

The typical guy always assumes it's a boy before knowing for sure. I wanted to say yes so bad, but I wasn't sure if I was ready for the wifely type life. "I don't know, Key. That's a big step."

He stood up in front of me. "You were already moving away to college. What's different?"

163

"You're different! This baby makes it different."

"You'll be okay. You can come home whenever you want."

"That's not the point."

"Well, what's the point? Tell me another way this will work." I didn't have an answer for that, so he continued. "Exactly! You think your parents want to take care of another baby if they aint got to? Come on, we can be a family."

"A family comes with marriage, Key." I was glad he wasn't eating or drinking anything because I probably would have killed him with that one.

"Hold, hold up, you losing me here," he said, taking a seat back on the sofa.

"I'm not asking you to marry me. I'm saying that I'm not playing house with you all the way in Miami. Who knows how you will act out there."

"I don't know what else to say. It's your call."

I sat conveying different alternatives, but the truth is, Key was right. I see it all the time on TV how men, even celebrities, end up in predicaments like this and look on. They could care less what happens until its time to go to court for child support. Here he is accepting it like a man, and I'm the one making it difficult. I leaned back in the seat looking up to the ceiling.

"Everything is just happening so fast."

He sat back up looking nervous. "You need to hurry up and make a decision. Did you tell your folks yet?"

"My mom knows, but I still have to talk to my dad. She was pissed, but after she calmed down, she said it's my life so it's my decision."

"Just like that?" he questioned, surprised. "That means your dad is going to hit the roof. I'm not trying to be around for that."

"You should have thought about that before you had your dick stuck all up in his daughter."

"It's gonna be a long night."

I popped up pulling him with me. "You right, so let's go."

He looked at me with one of his crazy faces. "Tonight?"

"Get up off ya butt, Mr. Tough Guy." He ran upstairs to grab his things so we could apply the last piece to this puzzle. My dad! "Don't go try to pray now. Let's go!" I ordered. "I'll meet you outside."

Chapter 12

DRAMA

W hen we got to my house, both my mom and dad were on the sofa watching television. I could see Key's heart beating through his shirt, that's how nervous he was. My dad smiled acknowledging our presence.

"Hey, where are you two coming from?"

I gave them a kiss with a blank expression on my face. Key also spoke as we took seats. "Dad, remember I said I had something to talk to you about?"

"Yes, what is it?" Key and I looked at each other terrified to death. "Skyy," he said, waiting to hear what I had to say.

There was no response. I was stuck for words and there were the tears welling up right on time. I was hoping they would work like momma said. He sat up tall and cut the TV off.

"Key, what's up?"

"Mr. Raxton, I think Skyy should be the one to tell you."

"I don't give a damn what you think, son. What's wrong with my daughter?"

Tears trickled after hearing the base in my father's voice. My mom got up and went into the kitchen wanting no parts of it. I couldn't believe she bailed out on me like that, but who can blame her.

"Daddy, I'm…I'm pregnant."

"What you mean you're pregnant?" His loud voice made me flinch and Key moved back in the chair. "What…" He grabbed his head in disbelief.

"Daddy, I'm sorry…I'm so sorry, Dad. I never meant to hurt you. I'm sorry…"

He shot Key a belligerent look. "So I guess I suppose to feel better because you came with her to tell me?" He was furious.

"Mr. Raxton," Key began, ready to explain.

"Save it boy. I don't believe this shit. PREGNANT!" He stormed out the house and slammed the door.

Key came over to hold me advising he would get over it. My mom walked back in the living room to join us. "I guess that went well," she grinned, making jokes out of the situation.

"Mom, don't start please."

"Girl, get up and stop that baby stuff. You already knew how he would react." She passed me some tissue. "Key, you need to go out and talk to him," she suggested.

"I'll wait until he cools off," he disagreed.

"Boy, go talk to him. This is what ya'll want right? Go let him know you're going to handle your responsibilities," she insisted.

"Right now…"

She cut him off backing him towards the door. "Go ahead! He's probably around back by the pool."

"If I'm not back in 'bout ten to fifteen minutes, come find my body."

"Bye Key," she said, pushing him out. She came over and stood me up. "Skyy, look at me. The hardest part is over. You told him."

"I know, but you didn't see the look in his eyes? Mom, he crushed me with his eyes."

"You're his baby girl. How was he supposed to react?"

"I'm just use to him hugging me and telling me everything is gonna be okay. Do you think he'll give in?"

She gave a disoriented gesture and joked, "Your dad? I don't think so." She smiled which made me smile. "Take a ride with me to the store. He'll be okay."

•• *Key* ••

I don't know why she insisted I talk to him then, but I would've felt much better with us all coming out here to talk to him. Hopefully if he sees that I'm a stand up guy, it may make him feel more secure about me being there to do what I have to do. Mr. Raxton seemed like the type that likes to read through people. *Time to put on a show.*

He didn't bother to look my way when he heard me approaching. "Not right now, Tykey."

"Can I please talk to you for a minute?" I decisively continued, "I know you're upset, but..."

"UPSET! You aint seen upset yet," he roared.

"Mr. Raxton, yes we made a mistake, but I'm here to let you know Skyy is not going through it alone."

He got up from the patio set and walked around the pool area. "That's all you young punks know how to do. Stick ya dicks in anything."

I couldn't hold in my sarcastic reply. "I don't consider Skyy to be just anything, Sir"

"I know that. She's my daughter, so do you think I want to hear you tell me it was a mistake? You ruined her life," he said curtly.

"Hold up a second. I didn't ruin anything. I have dreams just like she does," I reminded him then took a deep breath determined to get through. "What's done is done. Now it's time to discuss what we're gonna do about it."

"What are you going to do about it, huh?" he continued, not giving time for an answer. "Be around for a couple of months, then fly out to finish your career while she sits back here raising your baby."

"I'll do whatever I have to do."

"Whatever you have to do," he mocked. "What? Be a part time daddy?"

"No, be a full time father."

He gave me another repulsive look. "How you plan on doing this across the map?" I put my head down and listened before hitting him with the idea of her relocating. "You're talking 'bout being a father. I thought you had everything figured out."

"I asked Skyy to come with me."

He repulsively advised that was not an option. "You aint flying my baby over there with no family and nobody else to talk to. You can't buy her with your money and all your fancy things."

"I'm not trying to buy her. I'm trying to do what's right."

"For who? You?"

"No! For the three of us."

He finally eased up a little thinking about the life every father dreams of for their baby girl. "That's my baby, Key. I just wanted the best for her."

169

"I know you do and I want what's best for her too. That's why I want her to come with me. She can go to school and won't have to work."

"She only had a month to go and she was out of here."

"Skyy is still going to get a chance to do whatever she wishes. I promise you."

He threw another threat, "Don't hurt my baby. I'll kill over her."

"I love Skyy," I assured him with my deepest sincerity. "Everything is going to be just fine. Just give me a chance," I begged.

"You had your chance and you fucked up. Now it's time to fix it." He walked back into the house and went upstairs with no more to be said.

I grabbed a snack from the refrigerator and calmly took a seat on the sofa glad the discussion was over with.

•• *Skyy* ••

When my mom and I got back from the store, Key was on the sofa looking less tense. "I see you still living," my mom joked. "Skyy, go put this food away," she ordered, so they could be alone. "How'd it go? Is everything okay?" she wondered.

"I don't know. I hope so."

She gave a playful hit on the arm and headed towards the kitchen, "Could have been worse. I could be out there looking for your body."

As I observed Key after taking a seat, I could see less fear in his eyes. "What he say?"

"Man, I was about to slide your dad," he joked and we shared a laugh. "I'm serious. He's a piece of work."

I gave him a soft jab across the chin. "Toughen up chief, you got through it in one piece." Key stood ready to get ghost before my dad came back down. "Let me find out you really are a punk," I chuckled.

"Call me what you want. I'm out of here."

I went into the kitchen to let my mom know we were leaving. As soon as we pulled off, I bugged Key the whole ride to find out how the discussion went. He advised he didn't feel like going over it again and I had nothing to worry about.

"Did you tell him I'm moving to Miami?" I asked, giving a heads up that I had made up my mind. This was my way of putting it out in the open.

He looked at me. "When did you decide on it?"

"My mom and I had a long talk about it. She said she thinks that would be the best decision for the baby."

"I never imagined hearing that from her. Take her baby away," he repeated, surprised by my mom's intake on the whole situation. "Is that why you're going, because your mom said it would be best?" I gave dead air. "If this is not what you want to do Skyy, then don't do it."

"It's what I want to do. I made up my mind on my own."

"Don't get down there and be crying to come home."

"Don't do anything stupid to make me regret going," I warned. I needed some reassurance that I was making the right decision, but he didn't catch on.

"Well don't go then. Shit! I'm tired of going through this with you." We rode in silence for a few moments. "You want to get something to eat before we go in."

171

"Yeah, I'm hungry."

"Don't get all fat and shit cause I'll ship you right back home." I smacked him in the back of his head for that remark. "For real, my baby aint gonna come out looking like a sumo-wrestler for the WWC."

"His dad greedy so he'll get it honest." We both laughed.

"It's been a wild summer. I never had so much happen to me in two months."

"I know it's been crazy." He gripped me in chokehold with his free arm. "Where you come from and how'd you find me?"

"Remember, you found me," I recalled, getting loose from his grip. "Something told me to stay my ass home that night. Them clubs are known for getting people in trouble." We shared another laugh.

We pulled into Friday's parking lot on City Line Ave. As usual, it was jam-packed. "Damn, I guess everybody was hungry tonight." I surveyed the place.

"It's always crowded up here."

The hostess greeted us with a smile. "Just two? This way please," she escorted, grabbing two menus from the stand.

After we got seated, I went to the restroom. When I came out, I noticed Key talking to a tall brown skinned female. I wouldn't have been too concerned, but her beauty was somewhat of a model's, which made me curious to know.

"Who was that?" He gave the original *nobody* response. "It aint look like nobody to me. Who was it?"

"An old friend."

I was playing the jealous role already. "And what she in ya face for? Don't play with me, Tykey."

"Girl, do you know what you want? I'm not for the attitude, Skyy."

The waitress came over sounding all perky. "Are you ready to order?" she asked.

I cut my eyes at her and said, "No!"

She kept her smile. "Okay, I'll give you another minute." She walked off disappearing into the kitchen.

"You didn't have to talk to her like that. What's the matter with you? I'm not trying to have them in the kitchen putting nothing in my food." I ignored him. "Skyy, the girl was before you, okay?"

"I didn't ask you that," I replied, never looking up from the menu.

"You're so damn spoiled."

"I didn't ask you that either."

"What do you want to know?" he asked, ready to spill the beans. "Stop acting like a bratt." He began to show frustration, but I didn't care. "I went to school with her. That's where I know her from."

I didn't respond so he came to sit next to me.

"Baby girl, you're having my baby. I'm not worried about nothing else."

I looked at him with glassy eyes thinking, *suckerrr*.

After we ordered our food, we began to talk about options concerning the baby and different schools out in Florida. In the middle of a sentence, Key paused looking as if he'd just seen a ghost. I turned around and that ghost was the girl Tasha I was fighting.

"I'm not for this tonight, Tykey. She better walk right by us, or I'm a slide her soon as she stops."

173

"No Skyy, not in here and you not fighting anyway."

"Well, you better take care of it. Fast!"

Just as I figured, her destination was our table. "Tasha, do…" Key began.

She gave me a malicious look before cutting him off. "Look Tykey, I'm not coming over here with no bullshit. I tried calling you."

"Yeah, I know. So what you want?" he bitterly asked.

She was so calm my stomach started to bubble. "I have something to tell you."

Before continuing with her sentence, Tasha turned and looked my way again. "What the hell you looking at me for?" I asked, giving the same humble attitude.

She smirked and turned back to Key. "I'm pregnant!"

She turned back my way grinning. If she could have seen through me, she would've seen my heart hit the table. I stayed calm not giving her the satisfaction to suspect any pain even though I was steaming inside.

"Like I said, what you looking at me for? I guess that makes two of us."

I went on nibbling on my piece of bread like her words didn't crush me, and could tell by the look in her eyes this wasn't in her plan.

Key became abrupt. "Hold up! I'm not trying to hear that shit, Tasha. How I know it's mines anyway?" She turned her lips up. "You know up front I want a blood test."

I cut in. "No, we want to see the results."

She looked at me ready to explode. "This aint none of your business. Tykey, you better get ya girl."

The classy lady role was gone. I stood up daringly, "You get me."

Key pulled me back down. "Why you gotta come over here startin'?"

"I can't catch you no other way."

"Evidently, he doesn't want to be caught." I picked the bread up and nibbled again to keep me calm and collected.

She looked at me but didn't respond, then looked back at Key with her hand out. "Give me some money so I can handle the situation."

Oh hell, that was my cue. I put the bread down. "He aint giving you shit."

"Fine with me. I'll just keep the damn baby."

"We'll see after I beat it out of you." I went to get up again.

"Skyy, sit the hell down."

"Yeah Skyy, sit down," she mimicked.

I could have choked Key when he said he'd call her later so they can resolve the issue. She responded, "You do that cause we got some unfinished business." She turned and switched her flat ass back to the other side of the restaurant.

"What the fuck, Key? You just stick ya dick in anything raw?" I rolled my eyes. "What you gon do?"

"Handle it," he assured, with the money look in his eyes.

"What you mean handle it? She's probably lying, so you aint giving her no money."

"I'll give her a couple hundred to get her out my face. I don't care about that." I shook my head teary eyed for the umpteenth time that day. "I said I'd handle it."

We both sat quiet the rest of the night. My appetite had left when she did so my food was watching me. They say when it rains it pours. In my case, I got to be climbing a mountain in the biggest snowstorm because this is really getting ridiculous. Key paid the tab and as we headed out. I spotted Tasha and a friend staring through the window passing whispers back and forth. I climbed into the passenger side and gave them both the finger with a grin.

"Are you still going to my house?" he asked, pulling out the parking lot.

I was still upset and infuriated. "No, take me home."

He made a hard U-turn damn near jumping the side curb. "This shit aint my fault, Skyy."

"Whose fault is it then? Who fucked her raw, huh?" I leaned across the armrest to further voice my opinion in his face. "You nasty! When ya dick falls off don't say nothing."

"I see you aint tell me to use a condom."

"I sure didn't and look at me now."

"That's on you."

"On me? Nah nigga, the jokes on you," I replied, out of anger.

"What that mean?" I didn't respond. "Don't get quiet now. You got so much mouth. Yes, I fucked up, but damn I'm human."

"I was told when you make the same mistake twice, it's not a mistake."

"Then what is it?"

"STUPIDITY!" I screamed, in his face. "Just take me home," I demanded ending all talk.

When we pulled up to my house, I got out and slammed the door. "Don't be slamming my shit," he yelled out the window.

I turned back for and moment, then continued walking. The ringing of his phone echoed out the windows as he pulled off. "Who this?" he answered, fed up with everything.

"Are you still with your little girlfriend?" asked Tasha.

"Where you at, Tasha?"

She was happy her scam was going as planned. "Home. You coming over?"

"Yeah, and I want to see some papers too."

"I aint got to lie to you, Key. You aint top notch like that."

"You know what? I'm not playing with you." He hung up, but she called right back.

"You right," she said, "I'll just call you when I have the baby so we can set up a court date for child support."

He got quiet and weighed his options. *I'm not trying to go through all that, especially with what I'm about to be making.* "How far are you?"

"I'm almost eleven weeks."

"How much do the abortion cost?" He couldn't believe it the price she gave was so expensive, never being in this situation before. "Three-fifty! What you mean three-fifty?"

"You got it so stop bitchin'."

"That aint the point. I'm not about to just give you my money to put in your pocket."

"Just come over so we can talk about it."

"There's nothing to talk about. Call me with some better numbers than that."

177

"I told you how much it is, so what it gon be?" she said, trying her best to lure him over there.

"I'll be over there." He hung up and thought about it for a moment then called his sister, Sheila, for more information about abortions. "Sis, what's up?"

"Where you been?" asked Sheila, not use to him being out of sight for more than a day. I assumed that's why she didn't like me too much because I was pulling him away.

"Getting ready for this big move, but I got a bigger question. How much do abortions cost?"

"Who pregnant, the new girl?" she asked, waiting to say *I told you so*.

"How much?" he repeated, not wanting the speech.

"I told you she was gonna trap you, didn't I? I don't know how much cause it depends on how far you are."

"Like eleven weeks," he uttered. "And it's not for Skyy, so please can you just tell me?"

"Somewhere around about three hundred. Maybe a little more or little less."

"Damn, I thought that bitch was trying to get me."

"Who is it?" He moved the phone away from his ear after revealing the name knowing she was about to snap. She wasn't too fine of me, but she hated Tasha with a passion. "I told you didn't I?" she yelled. "I can't stand that whore. Let me beat it out of her. I'll do it for free."

"I just want her out of my life, *for good*."

"What your girl say about that? Does she know?"

"She was with me when the chick told me."

"I bet that winch tried to rub it all in her face."

"She did, but she got played cause Skyy is pregnant too."

"Umm, Umm, Umm…What am I going to do with you?"

"What am I gonna do with me?" he asked, wondering how he got himself into all this.

"Is Skyy keeping it?" He shook his head yes like Sheila could see it. She figured as much since there was no response, "I should have known."

"It was both of our decision," he explained, to get her off my back.

He informed her about the Tasha incident and that he was heading over to give her the money. She tried to talk him out of it, but he just wanted it handled to brush one less burden off his shoulders. Sheila pleaded for him to let her tag along and promised to be good. At first he decided against it, but knowing Tasha, she might have had something sneaky in mind, so he agreed to pick her up in the next half hour.

About a good twenty minutes after I laid down, my phone was ringing off the hook. I wanted to roll over and cut the ringer off, but this was the fourth time it rang back to back and something inside told me to pick it up. I answered thinking it was Key trying to make up.

"Hey bitch," a female voice snickered on the other end.

It was Tasha calling to fuck with me. I couldn't believe it was this hard for the girl to just disappear. I should've known because when the sex is better than great, females don't know how to act. One thing for certain and two for sure, Tykey Tyson was the truth in between the sheets.

"Who is this?" I asked, wondering how the hell she got my number.

"Your worse nightmare." I hung up the phone ready to go whip her ass for having the nerve to call my house. When my phone rang back, I was frenzied.

She said, "Why you hang up on me?"

"Call my phone again…."

She cut me off mid sentence. "Why you not with your man?"

"How the hell you get my number?"

"Don't worry about all that. My baby daddy gave it to me," she lied.

"Look you sick bitch…"

She cut me off again to give her reason for calling. "I wanted to let you know he's on his way to see me, so don't be calling his phone interrupting us."

"Bitch, I'm gonna fuck you up when I catch you."

"I have to go sweetie. I think I hear him honking. Tootles!" she blabbed and hung up in my ear.

I was flabbergasted at the fact of that phone call, and upset that she got the last word. I jumped out the bed like an acrobat and threw the phone. "I'm gonna kill that bitch!" I grabbed the phone off the floor and called Key's cell.

"Where are you at?"

"At my sister's house. What you screaming in my ear for?"

"That bitch just called my house and said you on your way over there."

"How she get your number?" He too was confused.

"You tell me."

"Skyy, calm down a second. Yes, I'm going over there to give her this money. That's all."

"I told you not to give her shit," I shrieked.

"What else you want me to do? Let her have the baby? You is trippin'. I got my sister going with me. No need for you to go or get all bent out of shape."

"Yes I do need to go. Where she live at?" He tried to talk me out of it. "Where she lives at, Tykey?"

He gave in advising to meet up at Sheila's house. I hung up in his ear and headed out the door. When I got there, Sheila and I barely greeted one another. I knew she didn't care for me too much, so I kept my distance. Key approached me.

"You're not fighting that girl, Skyy."

"If the bitch gets smart, I'm gonna whip her ass," Shelia butted in.

At least we're on the same page for tonight, I thought to myself.

The three of us piled in Key's car and was off. Sheila talked crap like she was big and bad all the way there. I wanted to see if she could back it up. Tasha and two of her girls were on the steps waiting patiently. When she saw me get out the car, she twisted her lip up.

"Damn, you don't waste no time do you? Did I get you pumped up enough?" she smirked. When she noticed Sheila come from the other side, her whole demeanor changed. "I don't know what you came for, Sheila," she nervously announced.

"To whip your ass if I have to," threatened Sheila.

"You don't have anything to do with this. I just want what's mine." She turned towards Key. "Give me the money."

"Show me the papers," he demanded.

She rolled her eyes. "I told you I don't have them."

I start smiling because I knew right then this was all a game. If she really were pregnant, she would have been glad to throw the papers in his face. But I played along with her game.

"Where are they?"

"I wasn't talking to you," she snapped. "You gon be mad if I keep this baby."

"No I'm not. You're gonna be mad."

"And why is that?"

"Cause you gon have to deal with me for the rest of your life."

"Get the papers, Tasha," Key insisted, trying to get it over with. "I'm not coming up out my pockets before I see them." He walked closer. "You think I came over here to play games with you?"

Tasha took a few steps back. "What you gon do, beat me?"

"No, I am." WHACK! Sheila punched Tasha so hard blood splattered from her mouth.

One of the other girls came off the step to help. I moved in and grabbed her by the hair. "Bitch, take a step back."

She tried to turn around and swing, but missed. Key grabbed her away from me and smacked her to the ground. I tried to get to Tasha, but Sheila wouldn't let me advising I get out the way. Then she two pieced Tasha again making her join her friend on the ground.

Sheila started stomping her so bad that Tasha screamed out, "I'm not pregnant...Just leave me alone...Please Key, get her off of me."

I stood there and watched the other girl still standing on the steps. "Get her off, Key," she begged, scared to move.

I walked up to her. "Shut up! You aint shit cause if you was one of my friends, I would beat your ass."

Key finally decided to grab Sheila. I stood over Tasha and said, "You better not call his phone no more or I'm coming back."

We got in the car and sped off. I looked back at Sheila who was adjusting her hair back in tact. "Why you beat that girl up like that?" The three of us burst into laughter.

"I had to cause if she would have punched you in the stomach, I would have killed her." Key looked back at his sister and smiled. "What you smiling at me for?"

"Nothing," he said, thinking she was finally coming around. "What I want to know is how did ya'll know she was lying?"

"It's a girl's intuition. You'd never understand."

We bussed it up all the way back to Sheila's house. When she got out the car, she turned and looked at me, "My brother loves you, Skyy. Don't make me have to repeat tonight's drill on you."

"It won't be as easy. Believe that!" I warned her and we both giggled.

They hugged and gave their goodbyes before Key came over to my car. "Are you going back home?"

I pulled him down to my position. I was sitting with my legs still out the car and spread wide open. "No, I'm going with you." I could see him growing through his pants.

"Well, follow me then," he smiled.

"Nope, you follow me." I closed the door and sped off.

We got back to his house and cut up. I never worked so many positions in my life. "Hold up Key, let me get some air," I exclaimed, coming from under the sheets.

He pulled the covers back over my head. "Get it later."

Suddenly there was a loud crashing sound from outside the window. We both got up and ran to see what it was. "Oh shit!" I exhaled, looking at his broken windshield.

"I know she didn't break my window."

"Oh yes she did," I examined, with my mouth wide open.

He threw on some pants and ran to the door, but she was gone and out of sight. He came back in and slammed the door. "She done fucked up now."

"Key, just let it go."

"What you mean let it go?"

"Just what I said. Please don't run after her now. That's exactly what she wants."

"I'm through messing with these stupid gutted ass bitches. DAMN!"

He walked back outside to cover the car window for the night. I tried to caress him when he returned, but he wasn't feeling it at all. "I can't wait until we get out of here to get away from all this drama," I said.

He didn't respond. I could hear him breathing heavier than normal. I continued to rub his back in silence falling asleep soon after he did. It wasn't over. I knew it was far from over. Especially after assuming Tasha broke the window when in all actuality, it wasn't even her.

Chapter 13

FED UP

The following morning, I got up early while Key was still sound asleep. I slid on my clothes and whispered, "Baby, I'll call you later," in his ear. He responded by rolling over the other way. "I don't know what you mad at me for," I mumbled, getting up.

I swung by Kizzy's house on the way home to tell her happy birthday. "Hey crippled, wassup?"

"Just getting the kids ready to take them down my mom's."

"What's up for tonight?" I asked, wondering if her and Kenny had plans.

"I don't know. I don't really feel like being bothered," she depressingly admitted.

I figured she was starting to miss Tyrik, so I left it alone. "Well, handle your business and call me so we can do something."

"Alright, drop me off right quick. I'll walk back."

After dropping her off, I headed on home finding my mom in the basement washing clothes. "Hey Mom, where's Dad?"

"I don't know. He left early this morning."

I was hoping he didn't wash his hands of me because I could never live with that. "Is he still upset?"

"What you think?" she replied, twisting her lips up in the air like I should've already known the answer. "He'll talk to you when he see you."

On my way upstairs, my phone was ringing. I skipped up two steps at a time to catch it before it stopped. I answered out of breath without scanning the ID. "He--llo."

"Damn, you couldn't call me to find out how I was doing?" Slim asked. I lost all the feeling in my legs and could tell by the tone in his voice he was pissed but trying to keep his cool. "What? Cat got your tongue?"

"Why are you calling here, Slim?"

"I almost died, Skyy. Did you set that shit up?"

"I didn't set anything up," I spat. "I didn't have to. Remember you tried to rape me."

"I didn't try to rape you," he laughed like it was funny. "Stop acting like you don't want this dick."

"Slim, please don't call here again." I started to hang up until he asked about Key.

"Is your boyfriend mad at me?"

The question had me confused. "Mad for what?"

"He got to come out them pockets for that window."

"You did that?" I was appalled. I couldn't believe he stooped that low with his desperate ass and was laughing like it was cute. "That was some bitch shit. Don't no dudes run around busting out other niggas shit," I said, trying to make him feel stupid.

"You just let your cousin know I'm gon get her ass too. She got my homie mirked," he warned, assuming Kizzy set him up.

"She didn't have anything to do with it."

"You heard what I said. Keep both eyes open."

I sat there listening to the dial tone for seconds after he released the call. *I don't believe he broke that boy window. I'm not telling Key that so some more shit can jump off.* I called Armani and she answered sounding like someone just pissed her off, but I didn't have time to ask who. "What's up, girl?"

"Nothing much. Sitting here watching TV."

"Slim done busted out Key's car window," I said, hysterically.

She got as hysterical as I was. "What? Are you serious?"

"Yes! We thought it was the girl Tasha cause we was fighting again last night, but Slim just called me."

"That's some real girly shit to do," she said, agreeing with my statement to him. "Did you tell Key?"

"For what? So he can try to kill him?"

"He might try to kill that girl."

I thought about it for a minute. Armani had a point because we did assume Tasha did it, but that's on her. "I'm gonna try to calm him down. I can't believe that fool."

"You sure know how to pick 'em," she joked.

We talked about getting together for Kizzy's birthday and going out to have some drinks, but Armani clued me in on why Kizzy was depressed. "Yeah girl, Tyrik called her yesterday crying to come back home."

"What she say?"

"She told him no, but I think she's gonna let him. She loves that boy to death."

I heard my dad calling me from downstairs but acted as if I didn't. "Love will sure make you do some crazy things. Let's go over there later to sit with her."

"Okay, I'll call you after my company leaves," she advised, regaining back the same attitude she had when I first called.

"Company?" I questioned, and then assumed it was J.J, later finding out that I was correct. "I'm not even going to ask."

When I hung up with her, I called Key to find out what he had planned for the night. He answered sounding like he was in a good mood and I was glad. He let me know he was down at the auto repair shop getting his window replaced. This was at no charge and the guy hunted down the glass all in one day, so I know he had to owe Key big time for something because people don't work that hard for no reason.

"Where you going next?"

"I don't know. I need to start packing my stuff so I can ship it out." I offered to help hoping his response was my help isn't needed. But instead he replied, "I'll leave some for you. Don't worry."

"I'll be at Kizzy's house if you need me. Today's her birthday."

"Tell her I said happy birthday and I got her later on the gift tip. I'll just holla at you in a couple hours or so."

"Key, please stay out of trouble."

"I'm not thinking 'bout that girl. She got that one."

My dad had begun to call me again continuously. I silently closed the door a little more to make it like I couldn't hear. I thought about confessing to Key about Slim, but was too scared to say it. "I love you, baby. I have to go."

After five more minutes of my dad's hollering, I went to the top of the stairs and yelled down, "Yes Dad?"

"Come down here! You can't hide from me forever." I slowly walked down hesitantly with the puppy dogface. "Have a seat." I sat at the other end of the couch opposite from him. "I'm not gonna bite you, girl. Come closer." I went closer and eased up a bit since he didn't sound that angry anymore. "So tell me, what's on your mind? Key came to talk to me. Now it's your turn."

"I messed up, Dad. Now I have to pay and suffer the consequences."

"Skyy, Skyy, Skyy, you just don't know," he continued, massaging his temple, "Whose idea was it to keep the baby?" He waited to see if my answer was the same as Key's.

"Both of ours."

"Are you sure about that?"

"Positive!"

"I'm so disappointed in you. I wanted so much more for you. If only you acted smarter."

"Dad, please don't do this. Don't make me feel guiltier than I already do. I let you and mom down. I know that, but I'm grown now and have to start taking responsibility for my own actions."

"You made a bad decision. We all do, but now it's time to live up to it."

"I'm sorry, Dad. I never meant to hurt you."

"You're not sorry, Skyy. You're human." The tears started rolling down my eyes like an ongoing faucet. "Stop crying, Skittles." He used his soft palm to wipe them away, and it felt so relieving to hear those words. "So, Key told me he wants you to leave with him. Are you going?"

"Yes, I'm going."

He slightly hugged me and held both my arms while we looked face to face. "My baby girl done grew up on me."

"You knew it was gonna happen one day."

"I never thought it would be this soon. When Key and I talked last night, I could tell by the look in his eyes how sincere he was." He lit one of his jewel sweet cigars and continued, "I believe he really loves you. He promised to take care of you, and in my heart I pray I won't have to make him eat his words."

In my heart, I too prayed that promise wouldn't be broken.

He took puff after puff. "Cause if he doesn't, he knows I'm on the first plane smoking." We both laughed. "I love you so much."

"I love you too, Daddy." I schemed to get out of dodge while the going was good. "Today is Kizzy's birthday. I'm about to go over there to sit with her."

He picked up the phone, "You just reminded me, I have to call her dad. You girls have fun. I'm about to take your mom out."

"Where?" I asked, being nosy hoping to get a doggie bag.

"Somewhere for grown folks. It's not for kids."

I giggled thinking about how my dad took my mom to the strip club with him once before and the stories she told me about it. "Okay, I'll see ya'll later."

I went back upstairs to call Armani with a boast of energy feeling like I'd lost a ton of pounds. She sounded like she was in the middle of a sex scene when she answered. "Why you sound like that?"

"I'll call you baaaccck…"

I had guessed right and hung up without another question. The next call I made was to Mashae to see if she had any idea what Kizzy wanted to do. Since I didn't feel like sitting, I advised I would pick her up so we could ride over together. I hopped in the shower and threw on some sweats and a T-shirt. When I got downstairs, my mom was back.

I swaggered over to her radiantly. "Hey Mom, what's up?"

She squinted her eyes curious as to what had me so cheerful. "Nothing much. What ya'll doing tonight?" I shrugged my shoulders. "Take some of these leftovers wherever you going so they won't go to waste," she said, passing me pans of food.

"I know Kizzy and them will eat it up when they get drunk."

"They'll eat it up if they're not drunk. All ya'll greedy!" We both chuckled. I slipped up thinking she knew about my father's plans advising they have fun. "Fun?!?"

She looked confused and I had the *Oops* expression on my face with my mouth covered, which made her dig for details. "You better tell me what you know."

"Dad is taking you somewhere. You better act surprised," I warned, so he wouldn't know I snitched.

"He always got some tricks up his sleeve."

"Well, I'm staying over Kizzy's. Ya'll can have the whole house to yourselves to run around buck naked if you wanna."

"Girl, get out my face," she smiled, taking my suggestion into consideration.

I bagged the food and was on my way over to Mashae's house feeling like it was going to be a good night. And how wrong I was yet once again...

I spotted Mashae trying to push her baby father out the door when I arrived. I don't know why, but it always seems like I'm the one to get stuck in the middle of a baby daddy dispute. She was yelling so loud the whole block could hear, "Get out! You get on my nerves." I took my time getting out the car.

He was trying to pull her tight clutch off his shirt. I walked over trying to play peacemaker and break them apart. He started spitting how crazy she was and how that's the reason they're not together. Mashae smacked him before he could say another word. I tried to hold my laugh in but couldn't, which made him more upset.

"Yo, you better not hit me no more, Mashae."

Again I tried to talk her out of the grip and break them apart before we had to roll on him like we did Tyrik, but he was a lot bigger and stronger. I wasn't even trying to go that route. She finally decided to let him go, "I'm tired of him. You need to go get a life…"

"Just give me my daughter," he demanded.

"Why? So you can just drop her off at your mom's and disappear?"

"Give me my daughter!"

She mugged him. "I said no. You don't want to spend time with her, so fuck off!"

"That's exactly what I be talking about. You crazy!"

"You think? I'm gonna show you crazy the next time you have my daughter around them tramps."

"See what I be talking 'bout, Skyy?"

"Don't put me in it. I don't have anything to do with it."

He flagged Mashae and proceeded to his car. "Don't call me later to come get her either."

"Whatever nigga. Be gone!" We went inside for a minute to give her a moment to cool off. "I can't stand that pussy. He always got to act stupid."

"Girl, it must be in the water."

Mashae's daughter ran up looking pretty as usual. Her long ponytails were dangling down her back with colorful balllies at the ends. She had one shoe on the wrong foot and the other one off. "Mommy, I want to go with daddyyy…"

"Go get your other shoe," she told her.

"Who's gonna watch her?"

"His mom."

I couldn't believe after all that work and energy she put into that argument, the baby was still going to end up around there after all. "You are crazy."

"Yes, I am. I just didn't want her to leave with him." She grabbed her daughter, "Come here and let me put them on."

I sat watching Mashae and her daughter wondering how I would be a few months from now. I rubbed my stomach with a smile knowing it would all be worth it in the end. She grabbed her hand and headed out. "I'm ready. Did you talk to Kizzy?"

"Not since I seen her earlier."

"I hope she feels better. But on the other hand, I heard you had a busy night last night," she smirked, aware of the fight, which Armani had already told her about.

"Last night was crazy. That dizzy broad was lying the whole time about being pregnant. His sister floored her. I didn't have to."

"Damn, I wish I was there to see that," she exclaimed, and then brought up Slim breaking Key's window. "What is his problem? He needs help. If you tell Key, you know its gon be a war of the worlds."

"I know, but I can't keep letting Slim try to ruin my life."

"What can you do? Q and them gonna finish what they started soon as possible."

"Well, I hope they hurry up before it's too late."

We got to Kizzy's house and Armani had beaten us there. She was standing in the doorway with a drink in her hand talking to some neighborhood guys. "Ya'll started the party already?" I approached Kizzy who too had a drink in hand. "Kizz, you sure you don't want to go out?"

"Nope, I want to stay right in here and get toasted," she responded, after taking the drink to the head.

I pulled the leftovers out the car without asking twice. "Well, cut some music on or something."

Kizzy was the first to grab the bags out my hands. "Your mom always hooking it up."

We sat, laughed and danced around the house all night long enjoying our own company. To be honest, we were all having more fun in there by ourselves. Every time we go out, we see the same lame niggas with the same lame lines.

I got up to demonstrate how guys are at the club. "No this is the best one. Damn Shorty, you wearin' that dress." I mocked the line all the guys use on me. We all were rolling over the floor. "I be ready to smack 'em right upside the head soon as they say it." I watched Armani stagger to the bathroom. "Look at ya'll all drunk and shit."

"Don't be mad cause you can't be."

"If that is how I look when I drink, I'm not drinking any more."

Kizzy got up and started swaying back and forth as she sang the words to Shirley Merdock's song *As we lay*. "This is my song. It's morning…A new day brings reality and we must go our seeepperate wayyyyys."

"Why do they write these kind of songs?" I asked getting depressed thinking about past relationships.

"To make us more depressed than we already are," said Mashae, also in a daze.

Armani came down the steps hearing the topic of discussion. "What happened to the days when men use to care?"

"They either dead or in jail," I commented, thinking of an old friend I use to deal with my freshman year in high school. We were sweethearts until one day he was killed in a motorcycle accident.

"No, they all gay," blurted Armani, plopping down on the sofa. We all start laughing and noticed a tear drop from Kizzy's eye. "I know you're not crying."

Kizzy was sitting in her recliner trying to hide the tears that drenched her face. "Why do I keep letting him do this to me?"

"It's not your fault boo. It's a part of the street life," we all agreed. "Getting hurt is a way of living. It actually helps us live better if we learn from the pain."

Mashae looked over at me. "She has a point cause getting hurt makes you stronger. You know that better than us all don't you, Skyy?"

"Yeah, I'm the best in that field."

Kizzy stretched out on the floor drunk as ever. "I don't know what to do."

"You have to do what you want to do. Stop asking us what to do."

"I want him back so bad."

"Well, take him back. You must not be that tired of it yet. Eventually, if the pain gets deeper, you'll leave well enough alone. All you can do is play it how it comes. But before you let him back in, you better get rid of Kenny. You know Tyrik is crazy. He shot at ya ass before."

We left that topic alone and started to dance around acting like clowns. "Tonight, we don't need any men. This is our night," expressed Armani, blowing the liquor fumes in my face.

I pushed her back. "Armani, if you don't get out my face smelling like straight up vodka."

"I'm trying to let you catch contact. It's Belvie. You know how I do."

I couldn't help but laugh at her. The rest of the night we reminisced about old times and pulled out old pictures. The vibration of my phone caught our attention as it skid across the table. Armani passed it to me. I answered happy to see Key's number since I haven't spoken to him all night.

"Why is it so loud? Who's in there?" he asked, jumping to conclusions.

"Just us girls."

"Yeah a'ight. We on our way over."

"No men allowed," I joked, to ruffle his feathers. There was complete silence on the line. I tossed my phone on the sofa and said, "He just hung up on me."

"For what?"

"They on their way over here."

Kizzy tossed it back to me. "I'm not letting all them in here. All I need is for Tyrik to come here and see that. You better call him back."

Kizzy was nervous at that point knowing how Tyrik pulls his Houdini acts. I couldn't promise her that they weren't coming for sure, but Key suspected we were there with some guys so it was no way I was going to try and talk him out of coming. I threw the phone back at her. "I know he aint trying to hear it."

"Let's just leave," Mashae suggested.

"Then he'll think I was lying. Turn the music back up."

"You always getting somebody in trouble," Kizzy angrily said.

"I owe you anyway," I smiled. "I didn't forget you set up that little shindig with Key at the M Lounge."

"Get over it! You know you wanted to see him anyway."

I continued singing the tune that was blasting out the speakers and danced to the beat ignoring her attitude and sarcasm. "Pump, Pump, Pump, Pump it up…"

"Can you make me another plate, Mashae?" begged Armani, stuck on the sofa.

"I'm not making nothing. I can't even see straight. All the food is gone anyway. Skyy greedy ass ate it all."

"I did not," I lied, with a straight face. I don't know if it was a mental thing or what, but I was getting greedier by the day.

Mashae continued to blow my cover, "I saw you make like three plates."

"That's because I put a little bit at a time."

*BEEP...BEEP...*came from the sound of Key's horn outside the window. I ran to the door as he was getting out the car. "Why you rush out like that?"

"Cause I have to stall you while the niggas hide under the bed," I responded sarcastically since he entertained the thought.

"Don't play with me." He pinned me against the wall. "Why are ya'll in the house?"

"Kizzy just wanted to chill, so we stayed in and they got drunk."

He threw his hands up in the air. "Aw, should've known they was drunk?" He peeked through the window. "Tell them to come out and play."

"None of us is dress. Look at me."

"Tell Kizzy to come here. Kenny got something for her."

I called Kizzy and she came running out knowing somebody had something for her. "What's up Key? Where's my gift?"

"I told you I got you, but my man over there waiting for you," Key directed, as Kenny got out the car holding a little bag in his hand.

I whispered, "What is it?"

"You'll see nosy. Are you staying here tonight cause we're about to go meet the rest of the fellas? If so, I'll call you in a little while."

"Yeah, I'll be here. Just be careful and stay out of trouble." I ended that note with a passionate kiss.

Kizzy came across the street grinning from ear to ear. "I guess that means you like your gift?" said Key, judging by the look on her face.

I still didn't know what it was, but anxious to find out. She pulled the gift out the bag. It was a diamond tennis bracelet with black and white stones filled all the way around. Kenny yelled across the street advising Rome called and they were waiting on them. Key placed another kiss on my cheek before departing. I continued to examine the bracelet inside and out wanting that to be my next gift.

"Look at that shit bling."

"I can't believe he bought me this," she said amazed herself.

"I told you Kenny is feeling you. You never take my word for it."

She knew damn well she shouldn't have accepted the gift if she planned on dropping him tomorrow. "How do I suppose to get rid of him now?"

"Your guess is just as good as mines."

We went back inside to show off the gift. Armani leaped off the sofa soon as Kizzy hit the door. Her and Mashae were peeking out the window but couldn't get a good enough look. "What the hell? Let me see that. Damn, I can't believe he bought you this," echoed around the room.

"Why can't you?"

"I didn't know he was feeling you like that?"

"You aint the only pimp," she said, smiling down on her diamonds.

"I see," agreed Armani. "If Tyrik see that, I don't even want to think what's gon happen. How you gon hide it?"

I wanted to know why she didn't get a ring on her finger today with all the crying and shit he's been doing. Something got to give and I couldn't help but ask, "What Tyrik buy you anyway?"

"I don't know. He tried to come over earlier, but I told him no."

"You crazy, I would have got my gift. All that bullshit he put you through," Mashae said, trying on Kizzy's bracelet.

I pulled out a blanket from the closet ready to call it a night. "The hell with ya'll. I'm tired."

"You not going to sleep. You better tell the baby hold up a second. We got to cut the cake."

Kizzy got sentimental. "Aw, you bought me a cake?"

"Yeah spoiled. It's in the car."

"We lit candles and played the whole song out giving a big group hug. "Happy birthday to you...Happy birthday to you..."

After cutting the cake, we all laid back and listened to Golden Girl cut up on Power 99 FM. She was keeping things hot and sexy with love talk and slow jamz on her *Power After Hours* segment. This was the first time in a long time we got to chill all night together. The things we been through as a team and the strong bond us four shared was unbreakable. With all that has happened over the years and what I was going through at that time had me thanking God for the *L*ove of my girls. I wouldn't replace them for anything in the world.

•• *Key* ••

I sat in the back of Q's truck dumbfounded. The blood from one of my best friends stained my crisp white T-shirt. Everyone was speechless at this point. I couldn't grip the fact that Kenny was gone. Gone? It couldn't be. My homie was gunned down right in front of me. How could I have let that happen? What kind of friend am I? I was dropped off at my car so I could get out of dodge and they could do the same. I gave a head nod to them all before exiting the vehicle. I felt dizzy and there was only one person I needed at that point. Skyy! I definitely needed her in my corner.

My voice was jittery and all shaken up. "Get your stuff on and come outside," I ordered when she answered.

I could hear her rumbling through the dark trying to find her things still questioning what was wrong. All I could do was demand she hurry before hanging up in her ear.

I had the seat leaned all the way back. My distraught look frightened her. Tears filled my eyes, but none would escape to show the pain. "Key, what's the matter with you?"

"They killed my homie, Skyy. They got my nigga."

It sounded as if there were a lump in my throat. She badgered me trying to find out what I was talking about. I reacted by punching the windshield with my fist, which left my knuckles bruised. I could tell she was scared to death unaware of what the next reaction would be. "They shot Kenny. They killed him right in front of me."

She was thunderstruck. It took minutes before making another statement. "Please tell me what happened."

"Just be quiet. Don't say another fucking word." I gripped the staring wheel tight and pulled off from the parking spot so rapid skid marks were left in the street. She begged for me to slow down before the police stop us, but I ignored her request.

"I don't give a fuck!"

"Key, slow down," she screamed, afraid for our lives. I ran every stop sign and red light we came across. "Key, slow the hell down before you crash."

I finally listened when she started hitting me frantically. "He died in my arms, Skyy. He died right in my fucking arms!"

Again she became speechless. I headed for the Marriott Hotel down by the Philadelphia Int'l Airport. After arriving, I passed her some money. "Go get us a room while I park."

When we got inside the room, I sat on the bed motionless as she begged for more answers. "Baby, please tell me what happened."

I got up from the bed and leaned up against the wall. "I can't believe this shit happened." I strategically punched the wall with the same bruised knuckles.

"Who did this?"

I ignored the questions once again and walked into the bathroom slamming the door behind me. I could hear Skyy through the shallow walls crying to someone on the phone. "Cut on the news to see if there's anything about a shooting. Tell Armani to call Rome and see if he's okay," she sniffled. There was a lengthy pause. "Kenny got shot, Kizz."

Hearing the words once again sink into my head made me quiver. I finally broke down in tears behind closed doors. Hearing the cries from the other room made it worse. I then heard the words again, "Kenny's dead." There was nothing more said after that. Seconds later came a knock on the bathroom door. "Not right now, Skyy," I advised.

"Please come talk to me," she urged.

"Give me a minute. Just let me be."

After an hour went by, I ran the water for the shower. I made sure to unlock the door before getting in. A cold drift seeped through the cracks of the shower curtain warning that Skyy had entered the bathroom. Her soft hands began soothing my back letting the soapy suds drip all over. I stayed posted with my back towards her letting the hot water rush down my face. The love was much needed, so I turned around giving off a long fervent kiss. It wasn't hard to express how much she meant to me, but when she responded, "I never want to lose you," my body went numb for a few seconds. We then made love as the hot water ran all over our bodies intensifying the sex even more.

At last, we both had calmed down and escaped into each other's arms. I began to explain step by step what happened.

"After leaving ya'll, we met up with Rome, Q, Chuck and a couple others to finish out the beef with Slim. Someone gave Q the heads up on the whereabouts of Slim's hideout, so he planned for us to roll up on him and finish what was started. Only it didn't turn out that way. When we arrived to the destination, things didn't go as expected because Slim was already aware of what was going down."

"What you mean? I thought Q had it set up…Who do you think snitched?" She went on not letting me get a word out.

"We know who it was. The only other person that knew what was going down was Tommy, and he didn't show up at our meeting point." I shook my head still in a state of disbelief that one we called our brother set us up like that.

"Who?" she asked, not wanting to believe the name I just said.

"Tommy!" I repeated, with the look of the devil in my eyes.

Tommy was my childhood friend, the one that Mashae was messing with. He wasn't as close to me as Kenny or Rome, but we were still like family. We all grew up together and would have never thought that one would betray the other. "Are you sure? Why would he tell?"

"Cause he's a bitch, that's why."

203

"Well, where is he now?"

"Floatin' with the fish where he belong. We found him after everything went down," I admitted, with a slight bit of heartache having to kill one of my own. "Slim threatened his punk ass and he gave in like a nut."

"And Kenny?"

I started to get that lump in my throat again with the mention of Kenny's name. "I tried to get to him, but it was too late."

"Where's Rome?"

"He was flipping out uncontrollably. His girl took him to her house."

"His girl?" she surprisingly blurted.

"Don't go there right now." I assured this was not the time.

"Well, did ya'll get Slim?"

"I'm not for sure. He got shot, but I don't know where he got hit at."

She rubbed my back trying to calm me ignoring the ring of her cell phone. It rang two more times before she decided to pick up. Kizzy was on the other end sniffling advising we cut the news on, but by the time I turned to channel 10, we had only caught the tail end. The media stated that there was a shoot out on 38th & Lancaster Avenue leaving three men dead and no suspects in custody. The area was blocked off with yellow tape, and there were chalked circles enclosing bullet shells making the street look more like a battle zone.

"Fuck man!" I shouted, now hopping back out the bed.

"Who are the other two they're talking about?"

"I don't know who they were. I never seen them before."

I flipped open my cell phone to answer the call. It was Rome making sure I was okay and informed me that Q and the rest were fine. We agreed to meet in the morning over Kenny's mother's house to pay our respects. I knew she was taking it hard with him being an only child. I rested my head on Skyy's chest as she rubbed through my hair, "How is Kizzy taking it?"

"She was crying. I'm just glad Mashae and Armani are there with her."

"It's not over, you know he's coming back."

"Maybe he'll lay low for a while and we'll be gone by time he thinks about retaliating," she suggested, hoping that was true, but who was she kidding.

I glanced up and said, "And what if we're not?"

She responded with silence thinking just that. *What if we're not?*

Chapter 14

TIME FLIES WHEN YOU'RE HAVING FUN

K enny's funeral was packed with everyone showing much love. Key and Rome put up most of the money making sure Kenny's mother was well taken care of. There were beautiful arrangements set around the room with dollar sign and RIP symbols scattered to represent. Both Key and Rome took it harder than expected, but still found the strength to stand and say a few words about Kenny at his best.

After the burial, we all went to Kenny's house to pay respects to his family. This was the first time in days we all came together after agreeing to lay low so things could blow over. This was the exact way we kept it between us for the next couple weeks.

*****

August 21st hit and it's been two weeks since the incident. Still no one seen or even heard of Slim. Key and I had seven more days to get through before heading off to start our new lives together. My mother and father decided to give us a going away cook out at our house with little invite.

I was in the midst of getting dressed when my mom burst through my door asking me to run to the market to get more hot dog and hamburger rolls.

"Mom, I'm trying to get dressed," I whined.

"Look, you wanted this cookout."

"No, actually you wanted it," I reminded her.

"Girl take your ass to the store," she demanded. "And hurry because people are arriving."

I got my keys and headed to the car, bumping into Key on the way out with a box of liquor in his hands. He tried to pass me the box, but I snatched my hands away. "Take it in yourself. I'll see you when I get back."

"I'll be back. I have to go pick up my mom and sister."

Key's mother, Ms. Pat, felt the same way Sheila once felt about me. To their knowledge, I was a sneaky and conniving female trying to win myself a ticket out the ghetto.

I couldn't help but to release my comment, "Oh boy, here comes the double team." I imagined them both breathing down my neck at the same time.

"Would you chill out. They're not worried about you."

"That's a first," I grimaced, being smart but he didn't pay me any mind.

I gave him another kiss before pulling off. When I got to the store, Jae was coming out with her head down reading over her lottery tickets. I snatched them out her hand to capture her attention.

"Skyy, where you been girl?" she wondered, being she haven't seen me since the birthday party.

"Resting up for this move. We're having a cookout at the house. Come by."

"You know I'm where the food at," she grinned, rubbing her belly. It seemed like everybody I hung around was just as greedy as I was. She looked at my stomach and smiled lifting my shirt a little.

207

I should have guessed my pregnancy was something that wouldn't take long to hit the streets, especially with someone like Tasha knowing my business. "Oh you heard?"

"Yeah, I heard you about to be a mommy. You ready?"

"As ready as I'm gon be. I still can't believe it."

"I heard some girl in the hair salon the other day talking about you and Key," she frowned.

I was curious to know what the hell they were talking about. I braced myself for the details.

"I think the child name was Tisha or something."

"You mean Tasha?" I asked, figuring she would be the culprit.

"I don't remember, but you never know who knows who. Girl, she called you a gold digging hoe," she cracked up.

The girl was actually going around talking about me to everybody pressed for the attention. "I can't stand her. She just won't quit."

"Don't worry 'bout it cause NeNe hit her and you know I followed up."

"Stop lying," I acted, surprised. "Why didn't you call me?" She gave me the run down on what happened and advised they had everything under control. "Ya'll two is crazy." I pulled the door open to enter the store as we exchanged goodbyes and said, "Let me go in here and get this stuff before my mom start blowing up my phone."

Back at the house, there was a DJ setting up while my dad stood in front of the grill turning meat. I snuck up behind him and covered his eyes. "I know my baby's scent," he smiled, turning to give me a kiss.

I set the buns up on the table and went upstairs to finish getting dress. *Cupid* was blasting out my speakers off the

112 CD. I was singing the words at the top of my lungs when there came a knock at my bedroom door.

"Who is it?" I yelled, cutting the volume down.

It was Kizzy and Mashae. "It's us, unlock the door," hollered Mashae. I took my time to let them in. "Damn, what you scared somebody gon come in here and get you?"

"What the hell ya'll want?"

"Girl, hurry up. We tired of sitting down there with them old people."

Downstairs, there was a light crowd gathered in the living room and more people out back. "I thought this was supposed to be a little gathering?" I asked, as my mom squeezed pass us on the stairs.

"Yeah, me too. You know when people hear free food and drinks they come running."

We watched through the window as Key and his mom pulled up and parked. "Here comes trouble," joked Kizzy, watching them get out the car.

She knew just as well as anybody else how much Key's mom cared for me, or shall I say cared less, because she didn't try to hide it at all. One thing I can vouch for is when it comes to Key being so outspoken with his mouth and ways, he sure enough got it honest.

"Keep quiet, Kizzy." I walked to greet them with a phony smile. "Hey Ms. Pat."

"Hello Skyy," she smiled, giving an unexpected hug.

I looked back at Kizzy and she was dying in laughter. I figured all this was a front for the family. That goes to show that maybe she does know how to act when out in public.

"Where's the food? I'm starving."

"My mom and dad are out back."

209

"Okay, Key go get me some cigarettes," she ordered, disappearing into the crowd.

"What was all that about?"

"I told you my mom isn't trippin' anymore."

"But a hug?" I asked, still shocked.

He shrugged his shoulders, "Hey look, she's just happy she's finally gon be a grandma."

Key left to obey his mother's wishes. Kizzy and Mashae were waiting for me to get back inside so they could mess with me. "Damn, you getting hugs now?" they joked.

"She must be up to something."

"She's up to something all right, the money. She knows she has to go through you now."

"Is that what it is?"

We continued to express our suspicions noticing Rome make his way up the front porch. He gave me a hug questioning Key's whereabouts. Armani must have spotted his car because she flew in from out the backyard. He couldn't take his eyes off of her, but refrained from saying anything good.

Armani was upset because he didn't acknowledge her and said in a nasty demeanor, "Hi Jerome."

"What's up Armani?" he turned back to me, "Tell Key I'll be back." He faced her before walking out the door with a smirk.

Key told me Rome was really digging her, but she was too caught up on J.J to see it. I shot her an evil eye. "What you do to him?"

"Why did I have to do something?" she spat, sticking her thumb in her mouth. "He went and got a girl on me."

"What was he suppose to do? You kept playing wit him."

"So what, he was supposed to wait."

She was really being selfish so I had to tell her about herself. "Girl, you got issues. Aren't you the same one that said you wanted to be friends? That boy got feelings and a heart just like the rest of us."

"You act like I hurt him or something."

"You did," snapped Mashae.

We were all upset with Armani for letting Rome go for J.J because he really tried to be there for her. Now J.J. on the other hand, wanted to come and go as he pleased hoping she'd still be there when he returned.

"She's right cause you did. As soon as I told you he was feeling you like that, you dropped him."

"Oh well, he'll get over it."

"You are so cold, girl."

"Call it what you want. I'll be out back with the food," she paraded back to the yard.

I watched while shaking my head and replied, "That girl is so silly." I then turned to focus my attention on Kizzy wondering why she hadn't told me Tyrik was home. She must have thought I would be mad or something. "What's up with you, Kizz? I heard Tyrik is back home."

"Damn, Mashae. Can I tell my own business?" she sucked her teeth.

Mashae was stuffing a hot dog in her mouth. "How you know I told?"

"Cause you got a big mouth."

"You act like I wasn't gon find out," I cut in.

"I don't care. Yeah, I let him back in," she nodded.

211

"I'm not coming at you, Kizzy. You don't have to get all defensive with me. You know whatever you like I love. That's how it's been and always gon be."

"He's talking about marriage. That's a start."

"About time," commented Mashae, clapping her hands.

Kizzy warned her to keep the remarks to herself. "I'll be back, that hot dog was good."

Kizzy was still upset with her. "Get two, and stuff them in your mouth to keep you quiet for a while."

"So Kizz are you happy or what?"

She gave a serious look sounding as if she hoped it would be forever, "For now." She leaned over and gave me a hug, "I'm gonna miss you. I don't want you to go."

I got up to go feed my face and pulled her with me. "I'll be back to get on your nerves. Then you'll be begging me to leave. Now come on cause I'm hungry too."

The DJ was spinning tracks off the hook when we reached out back. He mixed some of the old school with the new school keeping it versatile. My cheeks began to hurt from all the smiling I did as everyone gave their farewells like I was never going to return home again.

Ms. Pat spotted me and flagged for me to come over there. "Where is Key with my cigarettes? He needs to hurry up." She gestured for me to take a seat in the chair beside her and said, "I know you think I don't like you, but that's not the case."

I wanted to say aloud, *you could've fooled me,* but bit my tongue.

"I am just so protective of my boy. You know all the little tramps was after him when he graduated." She informed me as I agreed by nodding *yes.* "When I first met you, I did think you were after his money."

"And now?" I asked, anxious to hear her response.

"Now, I can see that my boy is in love with you, and from the looks of it, you feel the same about him. Just take care of him please, and my grandbaby," she grinned, rubbing my stomach.

She gave me another hug and I could see my mom staring out the corner of my eye. "I will, believe me, I will." I walked over to my mom cheesing from ear to ear.

"I see somebody's getting along," she smiled, considering how much I use to complain about Ms. Pat's attitude.

"Gatherings always seem to bring people together."

She began getting emotional, "I'm going to miss you, Skyy."

"Why does everyone keep talking like I'm not coming back?"

"We're just not use to you being gone all the time."

"Maybe ya'll need to miss me so I can feel special when I do come home."

She knew for sure she would be sick for at least two months after I moved away but replied, "Girl please, I'll be over it in a month."

Key walked through the door making his entrance known with a bag of ice in his hand. He threw it up in the air and said, "I'm here! Now we can party."

"Boy, bring me that ice," my mom ordered, snatching it out his hand.

He acted as if he didn't notice me standing there, "Sorry Mom, you know how the fans get." I made sure he did by kicking him in the shin. "Oh baby, I didn't see you." He picked me up from my feet and twirled me around.

"Don't play with me, Tykey. What took you so long?"

"I had to go get Rome," he advised, blowing his breath like something was wrong. "His girl found out he was coming over here and sliced his tires." I couldn't hold in my laugh. "That shit aint even funny."

"I know she aint worried 'bout Armani. She living with him so why she trippin'?"

"Go see for yourself."

I walked in the living room and witnessed off hand what the deal was. No more than an hour ago, Armani and Rome was beefing and now on the sofa all hugged up. "Wasn't ya'll just biting each other's head off?" I asked, jumping in between them.

"We like to play break up to make up."

"That girl gon get both of ya'll. She better not come around here with that drama."

"I hope she's gone when I get home," he responded. "She said if I came she was leaving me."

I tried to give him a heads up so he wouldn't be too surprised. "All that means is you're going home to nothing. You might wanna go check on your stuff."

"She's not that crazy," he assumed, and boy was he wrong.

I shrugged my shoulders replying, "Okay, suit yourself." I went to go sit with Key leaving that as the last warning.

The cookout turned out to be pretty nice lasting almost until midnight. Everyone made sure to hide or grab a plate of leftovers before they went home leaving us dry.

"Hey Skyy, if I don't see you before you leave have a safe trip. And no more babies," my aunt Tee advised.

"A'ight, Aunt Tee," I giggled.

She had her glass of CeCe in hand taking the last of it down. Everybody knew not to mess with her when she drank. "Jerome, don't make me hurt you about my baby."

"I got her, Ms. Tee. She's in good hands."

"I aint tryna hear that bullshit you spittin'. You heard what I said," she informed, bringing her glasses down to the tip of her nose so their eyes could meet. "Bye all ya'll hoochies." She staggered around to the front of the house.

After I brought up what Rome's house might look like, he's been thinking about it since. After dwelling on it, he decided to act, "Yo Key, I'm about to ride to my spot."

"I'll ride with you. Let me see if my mom is ready to go."

Ms. Pat was far from ready. They all were in the house talking about us when we were babies while getting more acquainted. Come to find out, our parents knew a lot of the same people and grew up around the same neighborhood.

"I can see ya'll are busy, so I'll be back for you mom," said Key, hurriedly leaving them be. "Come on she's not ready."

"We want to go," I whined, speaking for us all.

"No, stay here. We don't need no more trouble."

After they pulled off, I suggested we follow them anyway. I knew that girl probably had his front porch looking like something out of the projects because if it were me, I would've. Key and Rome had beaten us there. I scanned the premises without a sound surprised my assumptions were right. We could hear a female's voice

215

overpowering Rome's all the way outside screaming, "I'm tired of this shit. If you want the bitch, go get her."

"See all the confusion you caused, Armani?"

Rome was also yelling trying to get his point across, "Why you throw all my shit out like that? You always accusing me of shit I aint doing."

She yelled back throwing more things out the window at the same time, "You lucky you came home cause a lot more would be out there."

The high pitched voices kept migrating back and forth, "You know what, get the fuck out my house and leave every muthafucking thing in here I bought you."

Kizzy attempted to get out the car trying to get a better view. Armani was sitting behind me in my two-door Acura Coupe trying to squeeze out also. I tried to talk them out of it knowing as soon as Key spotted them, he would come out and get on me for coming around there after he told me not to.

"Don't let them out, Mashae."

Mashae hopped out anyway being just as nosy as they were, "I'm getting out too. I feel like I'm in the movies."

I slouched down in the seat when I peeped Key come to the door, but that didn't work with the audience leaning on my hood watching as if it were a movie.

He came over to the car groping, "What ya'll come around here for?"

A loud crashing noise came from inside from glasses being broken and more yelling, "Put me out, Rome. I want to see you put me out," the female tempted.

"Go tell Rome I'll put her out for him," said Armani.

216

"You keep ya ass right here," he demanded, while looking at me. "I thought I told you to stay home anyway."

"I was, but what had happened was..." I began making excuses.

"Save it girl, you're so hard headed."

Rome came limping out doing hurdles over some of his items layed out on the lawn. He was laughing like it all was all a big joke, "Yo Key, get this girl, she's crazy," He was out of breathe from the jog.

The girl came out chasing him with a butcher knife catching eye of Armani. "Oh, you brought her around here with you?" she asked, coming in closer.

"Yo chill, grab that knife Key."

I got out the car. "No cause if he get cut, somebody gonna get hurt."

"Why you disrespecting me like this?" she cried, which made me feel kind of bad for her. The truth was, he really didn't disrespect her like that, but looks are deceiving.

"I didn't bring her around here," he explained.

"Well, why she here then?"

"Ask me why I'm here," Armani intervened, hoping she would get smart so she could whip her ass.

The chick dropped the knife and headed back for the house, "Fuck you Jerome, if this is what you want, you got it."

"Armani, why you come around here?" asked Rome, now feeling guiltier.

"Why ya'll make me out to be the bad guy?"

"I told you I was gonna have her leave. I didn't need your help. Let me make sure she's not destroying my stuff," he sadly walked away.

Armani put on a pitiful puppy dogface like I aint know better. "Now I feel bad."

I responded, "Imagine that."

"You right, but it sounded good," she chuckled.

Key directed us to get back in the car and leave right away. "Ya'll seen enough. Go back home."

"But it's not over yet," whimpered Armani.

"I said bye. Skyy start the car," he demanded, in a striking tone not having it any other way.

I hopped in the car starting the engine as they followed my lead. "Key, you got twenty minutes," I informed, before pulling off.

Armani started to sing and dance in her seat doing the *wop.* "I got my boy back…I got my boy back…"

"You don't have him back yet. Don't get too happy," said Kizzy, reminding her that the girl wasn't gone yet.

"You wanna bet? I'll be the one cooking him breakfast in the morning. My brothers like him, so he's a keeper."

Armani had it hard growing up being the only girl out of ten brothers. Q was the only one by her mother, but she also had nine half brothers on her father's side. If the family didn't approve of a guy she met or was dealing with, then they were dismissed just like that. She could forget she ever knew them.

"It took them a while to approve this one," she continued. "But, I got it and I'm sticking with it while I can."

"Aww, look at everybody settling down," Kizzy huffed.

We all turned to look at Mashae advising she stop threatening her baby father all the time and make up.

"I'm not worried about him," she stubbornly lied.

"Your daughter is."

Mashae sat quietly realizing where we were coming from. She's been with her daughter's father since middle school, and with him being her first he was all she'd ever really known. It was definitely time for a change. Now that all the fun and games are coming to an end, she knew it was time to get her act together and bring her family back in tact.

"Listen to you, Skyy trying to play matchmaker."

"I'm not, but it's getting serious out here. It's time for us to grow up."

When we arrived back to my house, they were cleaning up all kinds of garbage scattered around. We pitched in and helped out confessing where we'd just come from and what was going on.

Key's mother responded, "That Rome is crazy, but that's my boy. My daughter knows his girlfriend, and she say she aint no good no way." After hearing that, Armani felt less accountable. "Do you feel like running me home, Skyy? I know Key is going to be a while."

"Sure, let me use the bathroom right quick." I was getting more acquainted with the toilet that I'd ever been.

On the ride to Ms. Pat's house, we drove back by Rome's house and everything was still spread on the front lawn. "She threw all his things outside like that?" asked Ms. Pat.

"Yup!" Armani instigated.

"I would have whipped her butt. Chil' take me home cause I don't feel like hearing my son's mouth if he see me 'round here being nosy."

"Me either," I agreed.

After dropping her off, we drove back one last time. By then all the lights were off and most of his things were picked up. I was hoping to beat them to my house, but wasn't so lucky.

"Where have ya'll been?" asked Key, assuming we went back past the house.

"Dropping your mom off. We took the long way."

"Where? Past Rome's house," he yapped.

I put my right hand into the air. "I plead the fifth."

Rome wasn't in sight, which worried Armani. "Where is Rome?" she asked, nervously scoping out the house.

"Calm down, Armani. He's out back. You got him, but you better not mess up this time cause he might kill you if you do."

"If it was me, I would."

"Skyy, you not killing nothing," said Mashae, getting her plate she stashed away in the cabinet. "I'm going home, you want me to drop you off Kizzy?"

"Yeah, let me get my plate first."

"Gotta feed hubby huh?" Key winked, also aware Tyrik was back home.

"Skyy, you talk too much," she said, sucking her teeth.

After Mashae and Kizzy left, the rest of us sat on the front steps for a while discussing our plans and move date. "Are ya'll ready for that ride?" Rome asked.

"That's gon be a long drive," Key confirmed.

"You should be use to it Skyy, as many road trips we took," Armani interjected, recalling all the PeeWee adventures we shared together from New York all the way down to Atlanta.

"But I was with you. He's a whole different story,"

They all laughed knowing it would be more than amazing to take a drive with Key for fourteen long hours and make it out alive.

Armani stood up holding out both hands to have Rome join her. "Come on baby. You ready to go play doctor?" She patted his butt.

I said, "Doctor? What type of kinky shit ya'll in to? Ya'll some freaks." Sitting there imagining the freaky things Key and I will be doing once living together was driving my hormones wild.

"I'll holla at you tomorrow, Key," said Rome, giving him a pound.

"A'ight dawg, I holla."

"You ready to call it a night?" he asked, giving me that sexy grin.

I wanted to rip his clothes off right there on the porch, but instead gave a gentle kiss and responded, "I had a nice time tonight."

"I did too, Mami."

We went inside to thank my parents for putting everything together. It felt so good to hear them tell us both how proud they were for acting as two matured adults, and thanked Key for being there for me.

"Don't mess with me tonight Key, I'm tired," I warned, as we drove away.

221

"You're not gonna be using the baby as an excuse all the time." He took my hand into his. "Are you ready for this move?"

I stared out at the streets of Philadelphia ready to put the past behind me. Although there was some good in them, there was always some bad to follow. "Yes, I'm ready."

When I walked through his door, it was a mess from the so-called packing he'd started. Boxes were everywhere making it hard to maneuver. "You know the people will be here in a couple of days to ship this stuff," he said, kicking one out his way.

"What you telling me for?"

"Cause, you still have all that little shit over there to pack." He pointed to the corner where all the odds and ends were clustered. "I told you I was saving you some."

"Hush," I said, placing my finger over my lips and fell down onto the bed. "I'll get it." As tired as I was I didn't want to think about any strenuous work, especially if I had to be the one to do it.

He watched as I scrambled to get under the covers and act like I was going to sleep.

"Okay you wanna play like that, don't ask...."

I jumped up and climbed on top of him before the sentence could end. "Sike, come here baby."

"Don't baby me now."

I started to nibble on his ear and kiss all over his belly. He couldn't control the squirming as I licked the insides of his muscular thighs and around his testicles. I stopped to look up for a moment, "I love you, Tykey."

"I love you too, Shorty."

"We're almost out of here."

222

He pulled me up so our faces could meet and whispered, "Almost, but not yet."

Chapter 15

TOO GOOD TO BE TRUE

I t was the next morning when Key started shaking at me disturbingly after being awakened by the phone. Armani was calling to tell me Rome's girlfriend returned last night while they were asleep.

"It's too damn early. What could she possibly want?" I asked, snatching the phone.

"Girl get up," she said, eager for me to pay close attention. "Why did that chick come back here last night?"

"Oh snap, are you serious?" My eyes widened as I gave my undivided attention.

"The bitch went crazy. She aint never say anything directly to me, but I still smacked her cause she started flaring on Rome. He didn't wanna hit her, so I did it for him."

"And you suppose to be drama free. Get the hell out of here Ms. Drama Queen," I snickered. "You should've kept your ass in the house and let him handle it."

"She came in here while we were in bed. Rome dumb ass forgot to take the key back so that's his fault. But she won't be back, that's for sure."

"Don't sleep on her cause you know how we play," I advised, to keep her focused.

That's one thing about females. They wait until they catch you slipping to retaliate.

"But that's not what I'm calling for. I need you to take me to the car dealer to drop my car off."

"Today is Sunday, aint they closed?" I asked, hoping they were, but I was a day behind with it actually being Monday.

"What's Rome doing? Oh, I forgot he don't have no tires," I joked.

I didn't know the speakerphone was on until he shouted, "That shit aint funny," from the background.

I ended the call after advising I'd call soon as I got up and situated. The sheets were thrown back over my head to block the sunlight that was beaming in.

"Key, don't wake me up no more please." We began to tussle in bed because he was now wide-awoke and ready to play. "Stop playing!"

He yanked all the covers from the bed. "You need to get up and pack some of this stuff."

"You get on my nerves," I yelled, attempting to piss him off, but was unsuccessful.

"I know. Now get up and get this stuff together." I jumped out of bed and chased him downstairs like a member on the track team. "Since you're up now, can you make me some breakfast?"

"No! I have some stuff to pack," I smirked.

There was no way I was going back to sleep, so I called Armani letting her know I'd be there around noon so she could be ready. Key came back up after cooking breakfast with two plates in hand. I made sure to give a juicy kiss.

Before leaving out, Key told me not to make any plans for tomorrow because we had business to attend. Whatever business that was, he wouldn't tell me. I tried to seduce him into confessing what the surprise was, but he wasn't having it.

"Tell me what I want to know, and I'll give you what I know you love."

"You better stop before Armani be mad at you for being late."

"Come on Key, tell me," I begged.

"I have to fly to Miami and I don't want to go alone."

I pouted and said, "You act like you had a surprise for me or something."

He decided to play mind games with me. "Maybe I do, maybe I don't."

I smacked him in the head and headed for the door.

"Hurry up back so we can go down to the place to make sure they have all our stuff in order for the shipment."

I complied by nodding my head and proceeded on my way.

I sat out front Rome's house beeping for about five minutes before Armani came running out the door. She was glowing with glee seeming to be more excited than she's been for the last couple months combined. "Follow me to my house first so I can get the paper work."

After dropping her car off at the Honda dealer, the service attendant said the wait would be a couple of hours so we went down South Street to kill time. The streets were full as usual with the normal police control directing traffic. We walked past Dude's Shoe store catching a glance at some cute multi-colored calf boots in the window.

"Look at those boots, they're cute," Armani said, dragging me inside with her.

I don't know why I allowed it knowing I'm not the best at window-shopping. I came out with two pairs of shoes and one pair of sandals. "Why you make me go in there? Key's gonna kill me," I grimaced, examining the expensive items.

"Well, that makes two of us. Rome is going to be mad too cause I just spent his money I was supposed to use to get him some fresh Tim's. Come on, let me get off of South Street."

We ended up going in about five other stores before making our way back to the car. I felt someone grab my hand as I was yapping away.

"Hey pretty, can you stop for a minute?" a chestnut-brown eyed gentleman asked.

He was not as tall as I would have liked, but he was built to perfection. If there was no Key, there would've sure been some of that.

I didn't stop but replied, "No thank you, I'm in a rush."

He was gorgeous and very persistent. "That's okay, I can walk and talk." Armani whispered to me how fine he was like I couldn't see that for myself. "What's your name?"

"Skyy," I blushed, trying my best not to be ignorant.

"Well Skyy, since you're so in a rush, can I just put your number in my phone?"

I stopped. "I'm not going to waste your time or mine."

"I guess that means no," he assumed as I gave the *get lost look*. "Well here, at least take my card and give me a call when you get a chance." He passed me a business card. "Nice meeting you, and you too," he smiled at Armani.

She snatched the card out my hand when he walked away. "Girl, let me see that card." She read the label out loud.

227

"Pretty Boy Ent. I thought he looked familiar." She recalled him by name. "He was down at Chuck's studio recently laying down some tracks," she grinned. "That's too bad for you, but not for me."

"I can see Rome killing you one day."

"I'm joking, I'm not gonna do that to my boy." She tossed the card in the glove box and grabbed me real tight. "I'm gonna miss you, Skyy."

It was a known fact that I would miss her crazy butt too.

The car was ready and parked out in the parking lot when we arrived back to the dealer. "Okay Ms. Daniels, everything is taken care of," the mechanic said, walking around the car.

"Thank you. How much do I owe you?" she asked, scrambling through her bag.

"Don't worry about it. Jerome already called to take care of it for you."

She looked up surprised and placed her wallet back inside her bag. "Oh okay, thank you."

He passed over the keys. "Let me go grab the papers for you to sign."

We sat out in the lot waiting for him to return. She was so happy she didn't have to come out her pockets, but realized how much Rome was trying to show he was there for her even if she doesn't need his help. "That's my baby."

"Now that's your baby, huh?"

She responded with sarcasm, "Yeah, I think I found the *One*."

We both giggled. I tried convincing her that it was time to stop letting the good ones fly by and falling victim to the weirdo's. "Don't screw up, he's really feeling you, Armani."

She exhaled before admitting, "I'm ready to settle down and chill since my road partner is leaving me." She mugged me. "Remember all them road trips we took?"

"How could I forget? We stayed on a mission."

The mechanic came back out with the papers for her to sign. Once finished, we hugged, said our goodbyes and headed in opposite directions.

Back at Key's house, he was passed out on the sofa snoring. I went into the kitchen to get a cold glass of water and threw it in his face to wake him. He jumped up to react, but I was gone with the wind.

"Damn Skyy, why the fuck you do that?" he snapped.

I laughed at him while looking down from the middle of the staircase. "It don't feel good to be woken up do it? Get your ass up."

He took his shirt off to wipe his face. "You play too damn much."

"You too." I jumped on him after coming back down the stairs. "I thought we had to go down to the place."

"I already went down there. Everything is set for them to pick up the furniture the same day we leave."

"Why not before? "

"Because, I paid them to have it there in one day."

"Okay big money. How about saving some of it?"

I thought I had the bags I brought in out of sight, but he noticed them and said, "I see you're not saving. What's in them bags?"

"Uhh, I have a perfectly good explanation. I was depressed so I did a little shopping," I explained, lying through my teeth and he knew it.

I went to kiss him but he pushed me away. "You're so full of shit. I'm going upstairs to lay down. If anyone calls me, I'm sleep."

"Except for who?"

"NOBODY!"

I looked up at him. "What the hell you yelling for?" He answered with silence and continued up the steps. "You on time out," I mumbled under my breath.

I sat downstairs watching TV for hours before being interrupted by the phone. I answered with an attitude still pissed with Key for raising his voice knowing how sensitive I am. He didn't have to yell at me, he knows I'm emotional.

It was Kizzy sounding excited in my ear. "Skyy, where you at?"

"What you so hype about?"

"I got to show you something. Where are you?"

I put a scoop of butter pecan ice cream in my mouth and replied, "Key's house."

"I'll be there."

"What you got to show me?"

"I'll see you when I get there," were her last words before hanging up in my ear.

Kizzy arrived about twenty-five minutes later glowing like I never seen her do before. "What the hell took you so long? What is it?"

"Damn, can I come in?" she asked, inviting herself inside. She couldn't hide her joy even if she tried. "Guess what?"

"Whaaattt? Stop playing and tell me." I was excited just by her enthusiasm. She held out her left hand showing me the rock on her finger. "Oh my God, Oh my God." I started jumping up and down.

"You're more excited than I was," she said, taking the ice cream out my hand to feed her greedy face.

"Yeah right, I know you almost touched the ceiling when he proposed."

"He finally did it, Skyy."

"Where is he so I can tell him how proud I am?" I asked, looking over her shoulder. "Kizzy getting married before me. Aint this some shit? How did he do it? Come on and give me the scoop. Play by play."

"I was in the kitchen cooking and he came up from behind. He turned me around and started kissing me, then pulled me to the living room." I was beaming from ear to ear as she continued. "He just started apologizing for everything. I told him all that's in the past and I'm not trying to hear about it."

"Just tell me if he got on one knee so I can clown him."

"He stood up and started saying how much he loves me and he's never letting me go again. Then he called Mookie out the room, and here his little butt come with a little ring box in his hands."

"That is so romantic."

"When Mookie looked at me and said mom this is for you, I opened the box and damn near passed out."

Kizzy and I both became teary eyed. "Give me a hug you baby. What you crying for?"

"You teary eyed too chump. I can't wait until you call me with the same news," she said.

"Don't hold your breath for that one. We got to go out tonight and celebrate."

"Hold that thought. Tyrik already got plans for us," she smiled. "I don't know where all this romance came from, but what I do know is if he keeps it up, Mookie is going to have another brother or sister." She glimpsed around the room. "Where's Key? I should go mess with him."

"No you shouldn't. Somebody done pissed him off, and now I'm pissed off."

" Well I'm going to find Rosie."

I gave her another hug and sent them on their way. After positioning myself comfortably back on the sofa, I drifted off watching reruns of Martin. It wasn't more than an hour later before Key came down bugging me to get up.

I turned the other way after hearing the sound of his voice over my head. "Skyy, get up. What are you down here sleep for?"

"Cause you got an attitude."

"Girl, turn around. I don't have an attitude." He scooped me off the sofa into his arms to carry me upstairs. "Come on up here with me."

"What, you lonely?"

"Yeah, so come on."

We went upstairs to cuddle. I told him about Kizzy's engagement and how happy I am for her. He was as shocked as I was knowing Tyrik from the streets and his background with females.

"It's about time he got his act together."

"He had to be the one ready. Not just her."

"His ass should've been ready."

"It takes time, Skyy."

"Time for what, all them hood rats to spend up all his money. I'm glad he came to his senses."

"Marriage is a big step."

"I know that!"

He turned the other way before saying, "I'm glad you do."

I decided to end the conversation after that comment wondering what he was trying to say. Just because a nigga aint ready to settle down, I guess we, as females, have to put up with the bullshit until they are. I don't think so! I will bring my ass right back home if he tries to pull that slick shit with me. *Hopefully!*

At nine the following morning, Key woke me advising that the plane leaves at quarter to twelve. I jumped out of bed upset that he didn't wake me sooner knowing how long it takes me to get dressed.

"You don't need anything, we're not staying," he advised.

"You said that last time."

"I have to come back to get this stuff situated. We only have five more days."

I was only in the shower for five minutes before he came and pulled the curtain back. "I told you to hurry up."

"I'm hurrying, dammit!"

We got to the airport just in time to check in and board. "So are you going to tell me now?" I asked, picking for information.

"Tell you what?"

233

"Where are we going?"

"What do it say on the ticket?"

I sucked my teeth and rolled my eyes upset for not getting my way. I spent the whole plane ride sleep.

We could feel the Miami heat as soon as we stepped foot into the airport. The same treatment came as before with the same limo driver. "Hello Mr. Tyson. The limo is out front waiting for you."

I can get use to this, I thought to myself.

Key passed him a sheet of paper. "Here are the directions to where we are going."

We got in the limo and headed out to the unknown destination. "Key, where the hell are we going?" I asked getting impatient. "It's been almost an hour drive so far."

He pulled me closer. "You ever did it in a limo before?"

"No and I'm not about to either. How much farther is it?"

"A few more minutes," he remarked, mad I didn't submit to his suggestion.

I couldn't tell where we were, so I sat back and enjoyed the ride. When the limo came to a halt, my heart began to race with anxiety.

"Stay here for a minute. I'll be right back." He got out and closed the door.

I peeped through the window as he was talking to the driver. When he came back and opened the door, I got out and examined the place. "Where are we?"

"Just come on."

I turned, and behind me was a tall heavy steal gate. "Who the hell lives here all secured like that?"

I followed behind Key as we approached a set of stained double glass doors with scary looking tigers on each side. I couldn't believe my eyes once we entered. The place was something spectacular I'm used to seeing on MTV *Cribs*. My eyes were focused on beautiful crystal chandelier hanging high from the ceiling. The driver walked from out the kitchen and cleared his throat to recapture my attention He had two champagne glasses in his hand filled midway to the top. "You like it?" he asked, amused by my reactions to the place.

"It's beautiful, but whose is it?" I questioned, still stunned.

Key took the glasses from the driver and gave one to me. "It's yours if you want it." My chin dropped and mouth fell open. "Pick ya mouth up off the floor."

"Are you serious?" I muttered in disbelief that this luxurious estate could be mine. I started to walk around exploring each room of the house. "Key, I don't believe you."

"Do you want me to give it back?"

"Hell no," I said, running and jumping into his arms. "Thank you baby, thank you, thank you…" I smothered his face with baby kisses.

"Go check out the rest of the place."

I ran up the steps like a young child eager to see everything. The upstairs consist of five huge guest bedrooms with two full bathrooms. The master bedroom was secluded off from the rest on another side. It was huge and beautiful containing its own bathroom with a Jacuzzi in the center of the room. Mirrors were lined at every angle. A pearl white marble floor covered the entire room. A double set of glass doors led to a spacious balcony overlooking a gigantic swimming area.

"So what's the deal? You want it or what?"

"I thought I already had it," I smiled.

"I still have to settle, but I wanted to see if you liked it first."

"How can I say no to all of this? But I do have one question. What's with all them bedrooms?"

"That's for lil man's brothers and sisters."

"*Brothers* and *Sisters*? Slow ya role." We both laughed.

He grabbed my hand and escorted me downstairs. We slow walked through the long hallway towards the kitchen. "Let's go out back," Key suggested.

I was very much amazed after touring the whole place. "Damn! Look how big this kitchen is."

"Yeah, you have a lot of cleaning to do." I waited for him to say he was joking. "Just kidding, but you better get down here and make some phone calls and do a couple interviews for some housekeepers and cooks."

"I sure will. Don't worry about that." He slid another glass door open. "Oh my goodness. Look how big this pool is." The outside reminded me of a Tropical Island. It was beautiful. The pool and hot tub was surrounded by flowers and a small waterfall. "Baby, how'd you find this?"

"The coach hooked it up for me. He said it looks like you."

"What's that suppose to mean?"

He laughed. "Ask him."

"This water is so beautiful. I'm ready to jump right in it."

"Well take your clothes off and get in," he suggested.

"Where's the driver?"

"He's outside. I knew you would want to skinny dip."

"You knew I would, or that's where your dirty mind was?" As soon as I took my last piece of clothing off, he pushed me in. I came up gasping for air.

"Stop crying," he said, still taking his clothes off.

"Look like I'll be at the hairdressers when I get home."

He jumped in making sure to give another big splash. "Like you didn't plan to do so before we left anyway."

He started licking my neck and circling down around my hardened nipples. I used the water to help me float up and down on his erupted man hood loving how the feeling made him moan for more. "Damn Skyy, this shit feel so good."

Up and down I went until I felt him clench on to my ass so tight ready to explode inside of me. He continued to moan in my ear.

"That's how you like it?"

"Yeah baby, that's how daddy likes it." I kept floating at his pace. "I'm 'bout to cum."

"I'm 'bout to cum with you," I whispered, in his ear to arouse him more.

We both had major orgasms at the same time. The feeling weakened my body and I began to tremble in his arms watching as his head detoured every inch of my body.

"You's a freak girl."

"I get it from my momma," I joked. "I hope these people don't mind me getting in the shower."

"Go ahead. I told you I just have to sign the papers and it's yours."

The sound of it all was like music to my ears. We got in the shower and headed back out to the limo where the driver sat patiently all this time. "You could have told him to come back or something."

"You think he cares about sitting here and still getting paid?"

"How much do they make anyway?"

"A lot, trust me."

I climbed inside and poured us two glasses of champagne. "Where we going now?"

"To the airport. This is the end of your day."

"That's it?" I yawned, sliding in closer to kiss him. "I love you, Tykey Tyson. Thank you for everything."

"I have to make sure you and my baby are okay. Just don't make me regret it."

I gave him an evil look. "No, you don't do anything to make me kill you."

"You stay threatening me, I'm starting to believe you."

"Please do. Don't make me have to show you."

We got back to Philadelphia Intl' Airport around 7 o'clock that evening. I couldn't wait to get home and tell everyone the good news, but when I got there the house was empty. I impatiently called my mom on her cell phone to find out where they were.

"Where are ya'll? I got some news to share."

"Out with Dad. Where have you been?"

"Stop acting like you don't know. I know he probably told you already."

"Do you like it?" she asked, already informed of the whole thing before I even had a clue.

"It's beautiful, Mom."

"I can't wait to visit so I can meet some of them ball players." I heard my dad in the background clear his throat. "I'm just playing sweetie. You know you all the man I need." I giggled. "Girl, my food is coming. See ya later bye," she said, ending the call.

I hated when she did that, but all I could do was laugh. I tried calling Kizzy and Mashae next to share the news, but there was no answer at either house. My phone rang reading Armani's name.

"I was just about to call you."

"Where you been all day? I called you earlier."

"We flew to Miami to see the house. I can't wait for ya'll to come down there."

"I can't wait either. I need a vacation."

"You always need a vacation. Matter fact, ya'll need to come with us. It's enough bedrooms for sure."

"Don't tempt me. I'll show up on your door step," she warned. "Just was calling to see what you were doing. I just dropped Rome off at the dealer to get his car fixed. I told him he better hope she don't come back and flatten them again. She keeps calling his phone crying."

"He did that girl wrong."

"It aint my fault…" She sang the lyrics to Master P's song like they were her own. "Hey, he made his choice. Time for her to suck it up and float on."

"Ya'll aint shit."

"I'll be over when I leave my mom's house. I'm about to get out of here before she talks me to death."

"I'll see you when you get here."

Armani arrived soon after our phone encounter. We sat around watching TV and old DVD's reminiscing on the good and bad times we shared together. "Girl, guess who I saw?" she said, looking a bit worried.

When she said Slim's name my heart dropped. "Did he see you?"

"Yeah, he gave me this crazy ass look. If looks could kill, I would have been a goner."

"Where the hell did he come from? We only got four more days to get through. Hopefully, he's tired of getting all shot up."

"Come on now. This is Slim we're talking about," she said, bringing me back to reality. "Key can play tough all he wants, but he better have a seat before he don't make it out of here."

I smacked her. "Don't say that shit."

"Inshalla! But I'm serious. Ya'll both need to fall back or leave early. Take your pick. Where is Key now anyway?"

I remembered him saying he was going to his mom's house so I quickly picked up the phone to make sure he was all right. Armani went up to my bedroom to lay down while I handled my business.

Key answered on the first ring. "What's up, Shorty?"

"Just checking on you. Are you cool?"

"I'm straight. What's wrong?" he asked, hearing the emotion in my voice.

I disregarded the question. "You still at your mom's house?"

"Yeah, what's the matter?"

"Nothing, come get me when you leave there. I miss you!"

"You're up to something."

"Just come get me, okay?"

"I'll be there shortly."

When I fell asleep, it was still a little daylight out. My parents came home finding me stretched out on the floor looking like I haven't been getting any rest at all. My mom nudged at me until I woke up.

"What time is it?" I asked, reaching for my phone.

"Almost ten o'clock."

I quickly arose to check my call history for any missed calls, but there were none. "Key didn't call me?" I snapped, instantly getting worried.

"I just walked in, Skyy. I don't know."

I called his phone but there was no answer. Armani was also still upstairs knocked out cold when I went to wake her advising it was 10 o'clock. "Damn, time went by fast," she stretched, surprised she slept that long.

I tried to call Key again for the sixth time in a row, but still got no answer. *Where the hell is he?* I asked myself.

Armani came downstairs to join the rest of us after washing her face. "Hey Auntie, hey Unc."

"Armani, where are you going?" I asked, jumping up ready to go crazy. Ever since she told me she saw Slim, I've been sick to my stomach. This man had an affect on me that was even destroying the way I comprehended. I rushed out the door before she gave her answer. "Come on, Key isn't answering his phone."

We hopped in her car in a hurry. She drove me past his house first, but his car wasn't out there. The next stop was to Ms. Pat's house. I got out the car to knock on the door although his car wasn't there.

241

Ms. Pat opened the door smiling with the least bit of worry. "Hey Skyy."

I tried to keep my cool. "Hey, I was looking for your son."

"He's up there sleep. I guess the symptoms are kicking in," she said, poking at my stomach.

I was indeed relieved but could have killed her for poking me in my damn stomach and I'm worrying myself to death.

"Where's the car?"

"Sheila took it. She had it all day."

I gave Armani a head nod letting her know everything was okay and yelled out for her to be safe going home. When I got up to his old bedroom, he looked so peaceful I didn't want to disturb him.

"Baby." I shook him lightly. "Baby, get up."

He rolled over reaching for his phone. "What you doing here? Is Sheila back with my car?" I guess my silence was answer enough. "Where the hell is she?" He got up and called her cell phone. "Yo, where you at?" She informed him she was only blocks away heading to the house. "Come on cause I'm ready to go home." He got up and put his shoes on. "How did you get around here?"

"Armani brought me," I said, wiping cold out his eyes.

I went downstairs to talk with Ms. Pat while he washed his face and brushed his teeth. Sheila came in trying to get out of dodge before he came down. "What's up Skyy? Why is he trippin'?"

"He just got up."

"Give him these keys cause I'm going back down the street," she said and in one beat she was gone.

I passed Key the keys when he made it down and helped him put his shirt over his head to cover the abs of steal he had going on.

"Where Sheila go that fast?" he asked, walking to the door.

"Down the street."

He gave his mom a kiss mumbling about Sheila probably not having gas in the car before heading out the door.

"Ya'll be careful out there," said Ms. Pat, walking us out.

"We will. I'm going straight home."

Key's house was still a wreck. We tried to complete the last of the packing so we wouldn't have that much to do come time to leave. "Did you pack your clothes yet?"

"My mom packed everything for me."

"Must be nice."

"I'm starting to think she's ready for me to leave."

"She is, she told me," he jokingly commented.

"Whatever!" My phone rang reading unknown ID. I answered but there was no response. "Hello." Still no response, so I hung up.

"Stop frontin' like you can't hear whoever it is."

"They didn't say anything."

"Make me hurt you."

The phone rang again and the number was still unknown. "Hello." Again there was no response, but I could hear someone breathing and laughing in the background. "Stop playing on my damn phone!"

"Who is it?"

"I don't know. They're laughing in the background."

"Hang up then. It's probably Mashae and them playing."

I hung up hoping it was one of them playing, but I knew deep down inside it wasn't. Knowing Slim was back in the picture, it was just a matter of time before he started his shit up again. We finished boxing and getting everything situated around two in the morning.

"You got a lot of unpacking to do."

"Me or we?" I asked.

"I'll be working."

"Well, you better take some vacation days or something."

"These are my vacation days."

"Then request some more."

"I'll be glad when they come get all this stuff," he said, throwing one of the boxes.

I pushed another out of my way. "I don't see why you waited until the last day anyway. They would've held everything for you. Where are the covers? I'm going to sleep," I said, tired of hearing his mouth. He threw the blanket over my head. "Do I get breakfast in the morning?"

"I don't know. Are you cooking?"

"You got a smart ass mouth, Tykey."

"You love it though. Don't wake me up tomorrow, I'm sleeping all day."

We both called it a night tired as ever. I was so anxious to get up and make it through another day so we could be one step closer to the road. But why did I have a gut feeling it wasn't going to be that easy? Why did I feel like so much more was yet to come? I fell asleep in his arms praying that everything would be okay, but I guess I didn't pray long or hard enough...

Chapter 16

RIGHT PLACE, WRONG TIME

Finally, August 28, 2000, the day had come for us to get on the road and leave all our troubles behind. I awoke to the sun seeping through the curtains and smiled thinking *We made it.* Two white male drivers arrived from Wayne's Moving Company on time as scheduled and ready to work. I asked the crew, including both Key's and my parents to come around 8 o'clock to help out, but you know black people, we're never on time.

Rome helped transferring boxes out to the truck while Armani helped me with the last minute clean up. Kizzy and Mashae conveniently made their selves at home watching us do all the work.

"What the hell are ya'll here for if you're not gonna help?"

They both stood against the sink demolishing the rest of the butter pecan ice cream I had left over. "We are helping by cleaning out the refrigerator."

I continued stacking boxes by the door avoiding a response.

Armani stood beside the 62-inch wide screen television and asked, "Are ya'll taking this?"

I cocked my head to the side. "Why wouldn't we be taking that big ass TV Armani? Nice try tramp. Hands off!" I pushed her back to work before she came up with any more bright ideas.

Rome came from upstairs with his face drenched with sweat looking like a buffalo soldier coming up out the desert. He asked where Key was and gave Armani a kiss advising he'd be back. Key caught him on the way out.

"I'll be back in a few. I gotta go take care of something."

"A'ight," said Key, directing his attention to the rest of us. "Are ya'll doing anything besides being in the way?"

"Yeah, we're clearing out your house. It doesn't look like you're doing anything but giving orders anyway," I said, placing my hand on my hip.

"Aint that what I do best? Bring the boxes from upstairs, and hurry up. These people don't have all day."

I kicked my 7½ shoe up in the air aiming straight for his booty. The movers came and took the TV out to the truck with Key right on their tails making sure they were very careful.

"Armani, can you get some of them boxes from upstairs cause these two aint worth two pennies?" I snatched a bag of chips out Mashae's hands.

Armani went upstairs to gather some boxes while Mashae and Kizzy were still in the kitchen messing around. "Hey Skyy," Key yelled from outside. "Bring me that box with the DVDs and CDs in it."

I grabbed the box and went out. He took the box from me and put it in the car. "What time are your mom and sister coming?" I asked, desperate for more help.

"Whenever your mom and dad pick them up."

"Come on now. They don't have no chauffeurs around here."

He smacked my butt and sent me back inside. As soon as I hit the top step, I spotted Slim quickly approaching and I froze, unable to say a word. *He picked a fine time to come with this shit,* I thought. As I turned around to tell Key he was coming, it was too late. Three shots filled the air, and Key fell to the ground. "Keeeyyy," I screamed.

I tried to run in the house and shut the door, but Slim was too swift. "Let the fucking door go," he demanded, using his strength to push inside.

"Help me! Somebody help me!" I yelled, trying to hold the door shut with my foot.

Kizzy and Mashae came running out the kitchen to help, but by the time they made it halfway to the door, Slim had already rammed his way in. I let the door go and tried to run, but he grabbed me by my hair.

"Come the fuck here bitch. Where you think you going?"

"Slim, what are you doing?" cried Kizzy, nervously half stepping towards us.

He started waving his gun in her direction. "You shut the fuck up! I owe you one anyway."

"He shot Key, Kizzy! He shot Key!" I was filled with tears and could barely get the words out.

Mashae was out of sight calling the cops, and Armani instantly dialed Rome when she heard the first shots fired. Kizzy tried to break for the kitchen to make it out the back door, but Slim shot her twice in the back. I screamed out her name after seeing the impact push her into the wall. She fell face down onto the floor. I tried to break loose but his grip made it so I couldn't budge.

"You see what you're making me do? Do you see, huh?" He began shaking me by my ponytail waiting for answers. "What are you crying for now? You making babies and shit! You think I'm having that?" He pushed me on the floor and started stomping me in the stomach. I tried to shield myself, but the kicks were too powerful. "Get the fuck up!"

He then pulled me by my shirt and dragged me outside down the concrete steps. I noticed the moving guys out the corner of my eye running down the street quickly like they were being chased. "You love him right? Come be with him," he said pushing me on top of Key's lifeless body.

I cried so hard after smearing my hands in his blood that it was hard to catch my breath. Slim gripped me harder and pulled me up. "Slim, why are you doing this?"

"Stop bitch'n. You sound like your brother!"

When he said that, I found it hard to breathe. I began hitting him outrageously, letting all emotions take over. "You killed my brother?"

"I killed his punk ass. He shouldn't have been trying to play tough guy."

I got weak and fell to my knees thinking about Samir, Key and Kizzy. "You sick fuck. Let me go." I tried to break away again.

"Your ass aint going nowhere. Didn't I tell you it wasn't over? I tried to warn you after I did your cousin."

I couldn't believe my ears. After all this time, he was the one that shot Q and Chuck that night outside the party. "What's wrong with you?"

"I warned you, Skyy. I tried to tell you it wasn't over in all my messages, but you just wouldn't listen. You always been so damn stubborn, so now its time to pay."

"Why are you doing this to me, Slim? Why are you…"

He cut my words short by pulling the trigger with a shot to my chest. "If I can't have you, Can't nobody have you."

That shot landed me on my stomach. My entire life flashed before my eyes. I couldn't believe this was happening to me of all people. Feeling the presence of Slim standing over top of me felt like I was bowing down to the devil himself. I lay still as I could with my eyes shut tight praying that he thought I was dead.

Could things have been different? Was this entirely my fault? Is this how the chapter of my life will end? All these questions wrestled through my mind. It finally dawned on me that all this time, he was warning me in the *messages.* If I would have just told someone about the messages, maybe things could have been different.

I couldn't see anything, but I could here *S*irens and five more shots rang out after Slim drifted away. My eyes felt too heavy to open, but I prayed he was gone. Armani and Mashae came running out to me screaming, "Skyy, get up! You can't go! Please get up!" Mashae cried, while rocking me back and forth in her arms.

Armani ran down the street to Rome where the last shots had come from. He had caught Slim walking away as if nothing just transpired, feeling as though his work was complete. Rome let loose every bullet available in his 40 caliber not caring if anybody heard or seen a thing.

He then ran down the street catching eye of Key and lost control. "Look at my homie. I don't believe this fucking shit!" he repeated, pacing back and forth.

Armani ran in and out the house checking on Kizzy and I dismantled about the sight of her two cousins slaughtered in cold blood. "Where the fuck is the ambulance?"

I pictured Key lying in that puddle of blood and Kizzy hitting the floor wanting to ask how they were doing, but couldn't find the strength to do so.

It took the police and ambulance about ten minutes to arrive on the scene. One of the uniformed men came over to check my pulse lifting my eyelids. "She got a pulse," the medic shouted, "Get a gurney."

While I was being lift into the ambulance, the cops questioned everyone, including the movers that found their way back after the police arrived. The media swarmed the place first chance they got after getting word that one of the victims was Tykey Tyson. I was rushed off to the University of Pennsylvania Hospital while each parent was contacted.

My mom couldn't function when she received the news, and Kizzy's mother wasn't doing any better. Ms. Pat was going nuts in the emergency room cussing everyone out, including the officers that arrived on the scene. Armani and Mashae sat side by side, holding one another in tears waiting for the doctors to come out of surgery with the verdict. The Action News played in the waiting room releasing the names of all the victims, specifying Key's name to make it more interesting. Rome sat quietly angry with himself for not being there to watch his brother's back.

We have breaking news out of South West Philadelphia in the Penrose area. There was a shoot out in a love battle resulting in three deaths and one critically wounded. One of the victims was Tykey Tyson, a recent draft pick for the Miami Heat. Second victim, Skyyzae Raxton, was rushed to the University of Penn with a gun shot womb to the chest. Kizzjah Raxton, was another pronounced dead at the scene. Kajuan Jackson, the last male victim, also pronounced dead at scene, was in his late 20s and goes by the name of Slim, a well-known drug dealer on the streets of South Philadelphia. No known suspects are in custody, but we will keep you updated when more information is available.

Rome looked away with disgust. Tyrik came flying through the entrance looking calm, but hardly collected.

"Where is my wife?" he asked, never showing emotion. He'd rather deal with it using violence.

"Who is your wife, Sir?" asked one of the officers.

He ignored the officer after catching sight of Mashae and Armani. "Where is she?" he yelled.

Armani put her head down on Rome's chest scared to be the bearer of bad news. When the nurse told him she didn't make it, he flipped out and punched one of the officers in the face for acting nonchalant about the situation. They hauled him off to jail for assault.

The police continued to question Mashae and Armani, but didn't get much information besides the fact that Slim was responsible for the whole ordeal. The two movers witnessed everything, but acted as if they didn't. They definitely didn't want to be the next victims after seeing the fierce look in Rome's eyes. There was no evidence that Rome was even there when everything went down, so he was out the clear.

One detective was determined to find out who killed Slim, but after finding out he was the reason behind everything, he gave up, feeling sorry for our families.

Key's mom was screaming out, "Lord Jesus, why you take my boy? Please give him back! Please Jesus, give him back!" The doctors had to sedate her with a medication before she lost control.

My surgery lasted two hours before the doctors finished. They let my parents know that I was in the Intensive Care Unit, still in critical condition. When Slim shot me, he just missed my heart, but if they removed the bullet, it would be a good chance of internal bleeding. My parents were the only ones allowed to come in and see me.

My father was holding up my mom by the arm because she didn't have much strength. "Look at my baby, Lord.

Please don't take her from me. I need her here with me," she cried out.

He rubbed her back promising things would be okay. The IV they had given me in surgery had me feeling like I was high off *e*cstasy or something. I couldn't even open up my eyes too much. Just as I tried, I got to see a tear trickle down my dad's left cheek. My mom once told me he was too hard for tears, but I guess there is always something to break anyone down. Watching me on my death bed was one of them. There were several different machines surrounding the bed, with that annoying beeping sound aggravating the hell out of me. *Beep...Beep...Beep...*

My dad noticed one of my eyelids slightly open. "Skyy, hey baby girl." He ran over as I tried to push the mouthpiece out with my tongue. "No, leave that in there."

I pushed it out anyway gently squeezing my mother's hand while listening to her soft cry. "Baby, you're going to be okay."

I could barely talk because my throat felt scratchy and my chest was hurting like hell. "Ki...zz...y," I said, trying to find out where she was. "Where...is...she?" My dad looked at me and another tear fell. I knew she was gone, and there went a part of me with her. "Slim, it..." I tried to explain.

My father interrupted by placing his hand over my mouth, "Sshh, we know baby. He's gone so you don't have to worry about him anymore."

I turned the other way assuming Rome got to him. It seemed like he had nine lives the way he kept avoiding death. I turned back to face them. "Key is gone, Mom," I wept.

She rubbed her hands through my hair. "Don't cry. Save all that energy to get better."

"He killed Samir. He killed him too." I noticed my dad eyes get wide and his face turned red after hearing that. If Slim weren't dead, he would have been gone for sure. I started crying harder, which made the pain increase and my voice squeakier. "It's all my fault."

"It's not your fault, baby."

"My baby…My baby," I repeated, thinking of my unborn child. "Oh my God, my baby." The tears started pouring from my mom's eyes. "Mom, please tell me my baby is okay." Her cry became intense.

"The baby didn't make it."

"Please…Don't say that."

The nurse came in when she heard my voice getting louder. "Ms. Raxton, I need you to keep this in your mouth, okay?" She placed the piece back into my mouth and checked the monitor marking something down on my chart.

My mother sat back down in the chair holding her head and still in tears. My father left the room to go get something to eat so she could take some medicine for her headache. I stared out of the window still listening to the sound of the monitor rang out in my ear. *Beep…Beep…Beep…*

Everybody close to me was gone. I lost Samir, my brother and best friend. Then Key and Kizzy were taken from me. Now come to find out, I lost my baby too. *I could've prevented all this. This is my fault.* I blamed myself over and over again. It was my fault because I allowed Slim to come in and control my life. The pain was too much to bear and I couldn't take it any more, but I did it to myself. The more I held myself liable the more the pains in my chest contracted.

I turned back to face my mom and our eyes met. I heard her say, "I love you Skyy," but I couldn't say it back. I wanted to tell her how sorry I was but couldn't breathe the words.

*Beep...Beep...Beep...*the monitor went on. *I have to go mom. It's time to go*, I wept to myself.

*Beep...Beep...Beep...*After that last beat, I had given up taking my last breathe just as my father hit the door.

*Beeeeeeeeeeeeeeeeeeeee...*was the sound that rang out from the monitor. "Somebody get in here!" he yelled.

My mom rushed back up to the bed. "Skyy, please don't leave me. Don't you leave me, Skyyzae!"

Somehow I heard her, but it was too late. I wish I had a chance to tell them one last time how sorry I was and how much I loved them. The doctors and nurses rushed in trying to revive me, but it didn't work.

My mom was screaming at the top of her lungs and knocking all the equipment over. "Someone get her out of here," the doctor ordered, trying to avoid her kicks.

My father was in the corner banging his head on the wall repeating, "Not my baby..." with a face full of tears.

When Armani and Mashae saw the nurses dragging my mom out the room, they ran up to see what was going on. They watched the doctors surround my bed and the sound of the respirator *flat-line*. Armani hit the ground and Mashae sat with her as they cried together.

Rome came over trying to pull them both up, but wasn't strong enough. The situation even made him weak. "Come on ya'll," he advised, with the nurses coming to help.

My Aunt Shena barged through the doors of the ICU overwhelmed with grief. Her eyes were blood shot red from crying the whole ride to the hospital. She walked around the nurse's station catching the tale end of the confusion. Assuming I was gone after seeing everyone on the floor in tears, she flipped on bystanders, nurses, doctors and whoever else stood in her path.

The doctors tried three times to resuscitate me, but to no avail did it work. My dad broke down and grabbed one of the doctors. "Do something! You can't just give up."

"Sir, we did all we could do," the doctor explained.

"Do something else!"

Security had to come in and restrain him. It was a sad moment for everyone. The nurses who worked that floor were in tears. The rest of my family came up to find out my status, but unfortunately, I was already gone. My eyes were shut, and I went on to be with my brother, my lover, my cousin, and of course my unborn child.

Who would have thought my life would have ended this way? Maybe if I'd never given Slim the time of day three years ago, I wouldn't be in this situation. Maybe if I wouldn't have fell in love with Tykey, he would still be alive. If Samir hadn't tried to take up for me, he too would still be alive right now. What if Q and Chuck didn't make it? Would that be my fault too?

Out of all the maybes and what ifs, it was surely too late. That goes to show, you don't sleep on threats and never take for granted who you are or what you have. Take them very seriously. I wish I had. I never would've thought the day I'd met Slim would have drastically changed my life forever. The one I came to know as charming and sexy turned out to be a total nightmare, and I thought he was the love of my life. Maybe all this was his fault for taking me too serious, or my fault for not taking him serious enough. I just hope all the victims would find a way to forgive me, including the ones that didn't make it.

"I will certainly ask them when I meet them up in Paradise."

Chapter 17

"UNTIL WE MEET AGAIN"

T he funeral was held on September 2nd, the same day Key was due to sign in for his first practice. Our parents agreed to have all three funerals in one, and as much as I thought Ms. Pat didn't approve of me, she agreed we should be buried together. She didn't even blame me for all that went down.

The funeral was packed with people from everywhere, including the media. The Miami Heat basketball team and head coach flew in to pay their last respects. As the preacher's words surrounded the room, cries echoed. This had to be the saddest funeral ever. They even prayed for my unborn child.

My mother didn't make it through the whole service. The medics on scene had to take her out for air a few times. Ms. Pat, on the other hand, was holding up pretty well until the media started asking questions, then she flipped out. Mashae and Armani almost knocked both my and Kizzy's casket over at the last viewing. There were a few nurses that came from the hospital having the incident make a major impact on their lives. Kizzy's mom made it through until the end. When it was time to take the caskets out, she tried to hold Kizzy back screaming, "No! You can't take my baby! Give her back! I'll keep her safe!"

Everyone in the funeral broke down in empathy. Jae and NeNe tried to console Armani and Mashae, but didn't have much luck. Tyrik too was able to show up after being released out of police custody. The officers felt sorry for him and sympathized with the fact that he'd lost his wife. He stood to say a few words about Kizzy and their unborn child. Everyone was shocked not aware she was expecting. Her mom took it even harder then. There were females that Key dealt with the past freaking out like he was still their man. In the obituary, Ms. Pat had me listed as his fiancé, and later told my mom he brought me a ring planning to propose at his first game. She let my mom keep the ring as a keepsake.

The crowd was ridiculous, so instead of having everyone at the house, our parents rented a hall assuming it would be that way. A few people stood up on the stage giving their respects aloud about each of us. The coach of the Miami Heat stood up with a plaque in hand for Key's mother and his jersey signed by the team. The plaque read, *#1 ROOKIE FOR 2000-2001. TYKEY TYSON. GONE BUT WILL NEVER BE FORGOTTEN.* Ms. Pat held the plaque up with pride grinning from ear to ear. The joyful expression she expressed brought a smile to everyone else's face.

After time went on, my mother did get herself together making it through the tough times with my father by her side. Armani and Mashae visited on a regular basis every time they got a chance. Mashae decided to make amends with her daughter's father realizing life is too short, and planned to get married some time soon. Armani and Rome grew closer after they found out there was something baking in the oven, and it wasn't food. They planned to name the baby after Key if it was a boy, and Kizae if it was a girl. They were talking about marriage, but taking things one day at a time. Kizzy's mom still had two younger children to look after, so she pulled herself together for them both. Ms. Pat coped well enough, but being fed up with the city life, she and Sheila decided to move to Miami in the house that Key settled on. Some of the money they were rewarded from Key's life insurance went to a foundation set up in his name, which was a youth basketball camp. They visited home often, but didn't plan on returning.

As for Slim, everyone cared less that he was out of the picture believing he'd got exactly what he deserved.

And that was the final chapter of my life!

A novel by Nyema

Just when you think marriage is tough… It gets worse…

"Deceitful Obsession" takes you on a journey inside a circle filled with misery, disloyalty and pain.

-Kassim, a young businessman from Philadelphia, has been married for almost a year and still can't define commitment. After meeting Sherae he falls in deep, but soon their sexual escapades become a hassle when feelings start to surface and DEATH almost crosses his path.

-Takyah, his beautiful and loyal wife, stands by his side until she can't take it any more. After her kindness is taken for weakness for so long, her mission becomes revenge. Assuming the best way to break a guy's heart is by sleeping with the enemy, she puts that option to the test.

-Sherae, a top notch model from Chicago, is use to getting any and everything she wants. When Kassim makes it perfectly clear that his family comes first, she braces herself and dives in for the challenge. Obsession takes control over her mind bringing total chaos into their world. In the end, she believes that she and Kassim are meant to be together, so it became her job to make that happen by any means necessary…Even if it means her finger on the trigger.

Look Out For

Deceitful Obsession

COMING SOON…

Sneak Peak following

DECEITFUL OBSESSION

Time to Pay The Piper

"I can't believe this shit! That girl was all up in my face and had the nerve to be all friendly wit my muthafuckin' daughter knowing damn well she was fuckin' my husband!?!" growled Kay, as tears trickled down her cheeks.

"I'm sorry, baby. I swear I never meant for this to happen."

"You're always sorry. I'm sick of it and I'm sick of you…" she yelled, continuously.

He couldn't blame her for how she felt at that moment. After all these years he'd successfully kept drama away from home, but now it was deeper. Assuming Juan, his supposed to be hommie, had something to do with it made Kassim more furious.

He arose from the chair. "I don't know what to say, Kay. I say the same thing every time, but I mean it this time. You know I've been trying really hard to keep things straight. I'm doing all I can to keep my family together, but I can't take back things I did in the past. That's just the way it is. If I could I would, but I can't."

Kay listened as the tears sprinkled like an ongoing faucet. "So what is she doing with Juan? Ya'll play pass around when ya done with 'em?"

"I don't know what she's doing with Juan and frankly I don't care. What I do want to know is if he had something to do with that box that came to the house…"

261

"You need to learn how to pick your fucking friends," she interrupted. "Now what? Do you think I'm staying here with people knowing where I live we can't even trust?"

"I'll take care of it, Kay. I'll handle it."

"You can't handle shit. You can't even handle the bitches you're fucking so how do you think you can handle a nigga?" The fire of her tongue fueled Kassim's face. "This nigga be around you every day counting your money, handling all your business, taking your personal calls, and a bunch of other shit and come to find out you can't trust him. I thought you of all people would be more on your toes."

Kassim was so fed up with everything he snapped back taking his frustrations out on her. "Let me fucking handle it. Damn! Go ahead with all that bullshit right now. I'm trying to think." He pushed her out his way.

With his back to her she yelled, "I fucking hate you. I can't stand your ass. You can't never look me in the eye when you're wrong."

Kassim stopped in his tracks to show some sincerity. "Kay, please just give me a minute to think."

"You want to think, right?" she snarled, about to let the cat out the bag. "Well, think about how he's fucking both of your bitches. Think about that!" She gave a devilish grin awaiting his reply.

Kassim's eyes opened so wide they could have popped out his head. He stumbled on his words thinking he'd heard wrong. "What!?! Both of my bitches!?!" he repeated, backing Kay into a corner. "Are you fucking that nigga?"

"You heard me. Both of ya bitch…"

Kassim fist covered her fragile lips with a harsh blow before the last letters could part her tongue. Kay fell to the floor to shield her face with the taste of blood.

262

"You fucked that nigga?" he questioned, demanding an answer. "Kay, please don't tell me that." His voice became timid hoping his wife was speaking out of anger, but she never responded being ashamed of her actions. After all the pain Kassim ever caused, the tables had turned indeed.

He stared down at her while she sat on the floor in tears realizing this was no joke. Kay could hear him breathing so hard like he was about to explode. Not once did she look up to meet his eyes. Without saying another word, he left the room and went upstairs. A few minutes later, he stormed back downstairs and headed straight out the front door. Kay sobbingly picked herself up from the floor to run behind him.

"Kassim, please don't leave me. Please!" she begged, screaming for him to come back. He paid her no mind, got into the car and pulled off.

Kay stood in the doorway crying dreadfully. When she went inside to the bathroom to clean herself up, it dawned on her that he was on his way to find Juan.

"Oh my God! He's gon kill 'em." Kay grabbed her keys and rushed out the door hoping and praying that time would be on her side.

263

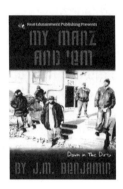

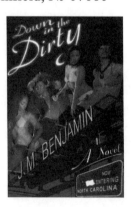
264